Rofy #22
S

Comfort and Joy

Dana R. Lynn

AnniesFiction.com

Books in The Inn at Magnolia Harbor series

Library of Congress-in-Publication Data
Comfort and Joy / by Dana R. Lynn
p. cm.
I. Title
                              2020949487

AnniesFiction.com
(800) 282-6643
The Inn at Magnolia Harbor™
Series Creator: Shari Lohner
Editor: Lorie Jones
Cover Illustrator: Bonnie Leick

10 11 12 13 14 | Printed in China | 9 8 7 6 5 4 3 2 1

Grace

Humming a Christmas carol, Grace Porter headed toward the kitchen in the Magnolia Harbor Inn with Winston, her shih tzu mix, at her heels. As she walked through the foyer of the bed-and-breakfast she owned with her younger sister, Charlotte Wylde, she admired the large Christmas tree and its twinkling lights. She loved the holidays. The sights, the smells of baking in the air, the music—everything about the season appealed to her.

Charlotte was removing a pan of cinnamon rolls from the oven, and the enticing aroma wafted through the air.

Grace breathed in the scent deeply. No one made cinnamon rolls like Charlotte. "They smell marvelous."

"Thanks." Charlotte set the pan on top of the stove. "I'm trying a new recipe to see if it will work in a cookbook." She smiled at her sister. "If you're nice to me, I'll let you be one of my taste testers."

Charlotte was a fantastic chef, and she had written several best-selling cookbooks. She was always experimenting with recipes to include in future volumes.

Grace laughed. "I can be nice if it gets me one of those."

Charlotte drizzled frosting over the hot rolls. She grabbed a plate, placed one of the sweet pastries on it, and handed it to her sister with a fork. "It's really sticky," she warned.

"Please. If it's not sticky, then it wasn't made right." Grace took a bite and rolled her eyes heavenward. It was scrumptious. "I think it'll do," she teased.

Charlotte helped herself to a roll and poured two cups of coffee.

They sat down at the island with their snacks, and Winston stretched out on the floor for a nap.

Charlotte sampled the roll. "It needs a bit more cinnamon."

As Grace took a sip of coffee, she remembered something. "Why are you still here? I thought you had plans with Dean this afternoon."

Dean Bradley was the chef and co-owner of The Tidewater, a trendy restaurant and inn on the other side of Lake Haven. Charlotte and Dean had been professional rivals, and their relationship had gotten off to a rocky start. Fortunately, they'd resolved their issues, and they had been dating for almost a year. It amused Grace that the couple maintained a friendly rivalry about their cooking.

"We were planning on meeting," Charlotte replied. "But they were short-staffed today, so he's staying at the restaurant until seven. We'll get together this evening for a late dinner and maybe a movie."

"Sounds like a good plan," Grace said. She was glad that Charlotte and Dean were making time for each other when they were both so busy.

"What about you?" Charlotte asked. "Do you and Spencer have plans anytime in the near future?"

Grace grimaced. "No. I haven't seen him in more than a week."

Spencer Lewis was a retired intelligence analyst for the FBI, and he lived on a pecan farm adjacent to the inn. Grace and Spencer had become good friends when he'd moved to town. Their friendship had blossomed into romance, and they'd been happily dating for the past few months.

Grace had never expected to find romance again. Her husband, Hank Porter, had presumably died in a train accident in Europe more than twenty years ago, and she'd raised their son, Jake, alone. She frowned as she recalled how Hank had showed up on her doorstop last spring, eager to worm his way back into their lives. It turned out that Hank had started a new life after he'd supposedly been killed, and he'd become a thief. Grace had severed all ties with him, but he'd already done damage to her heart. Damage that had nearly destroyed her relationship with Spencer.

"Are you all right?" Charlotte asked.

Grace shook herself out of her reverie. "Sorry. Off in my own little world." She shoved her distressing thoughts away. Hank had stolen too much of her life. She wouldn't let him take any more. "Do you need a hand with anything?"

"I'm good," Charlotte said. "I have one more recipe to try for hospitality hour, and then I'll be done."

"We'll have a smaller crowd this evening," Grace said. "The Smiths canceled their reservation."

"Oh no. What happened?"

"They both came down with the flu," Grace said.

"What a shame," Charlotte said. "I hope they recover by Christmas."

"Me too," Grace said. "Fortunately, the rest of the suites are still booked. Charles Johnston is checking in today, and the other guests are leaving tomorrow morning."

"Just in time for our new guests to get here," Charlotte remarked.

Four doctors were scheduled to arrive tomorrow for a medical conference starting on Tuesday and culminating Friday evening with a Christmas party in the renovated barn on the grounds of the inn. The speakers and other attendees were staying at The Tidewater and various hotels in the area.

"Yes, Howard and Wanda Reeves, Sam Matthews, and Alyssa Larson," Grace said.

The sisters chatted for a few more minutes as they finished their cinnamon rolls and coffee.

Charlotte cleared the dishes, then began removing ingredients from the fridge.

"Call me if you need help." Grace reached down to pat Winston, who was still stretched out on the floor. "Come on. Let's get out of the chef's hair."

Charlotte waved them off, laughing.

Marcie

Marcie O'Connor had never been the kind of person to make impulsive decisions. She was a planner, and she consistently jotted down her schedule and all her tasks in her journal. She found great satisfaction in checking the box next to each item after she completed it.

In addition to her appointments and to-do list, Marcie kept a meticulous log of every detail of her life, including the food she ate for each meal, the outfit and accessories she wore, and the books she wanted to read.

Marcie enjoyed carefully planning her life. She was comforted by her orderly days as an attorney at a respected law firm, and she looked forward to marrying her coworker and fiancé, Brian Dawson.

But all that had changed a few weeks ago when Marcie had lost her hearing. Everything that she had worked so hard for had vanished. Things that she had taken for granted had become insurmountable mountains. Brian had broken their engagement so quickly that it had left her breathless, and he'd even tried to destroy her career in the process.

This past Friday, Marcie had finally had enough. With her life spinning out of control, she had made a rare and spontaneous decision and asked her boss for a leave of absence from her job. He'd told her to be back in two weeks, and then they'd talk.

When she had walked out of the office, her car had been covered with a thick layer of ice, and the roads glistened with more of the same. She had gone home to her small apartment in Naperville, a bustling suburb of Chicago.

After tossing some clothes haphazardly into a bag, she'd headed south with no real destination in mind. She wanted to go somewhere warmer. Somewhere she could hide for a week while she figured out what to do next.

That was two days ago. This morning, she'd attended a church service in North Carolina, and she'd been comforted by her anonymity. However, she'd made the mistake of sitting in the back, so she hadn't been able to understand the pastor's sermon. She'd slipped out of her pew and walked out before the service was over. She'd entered South Carolina right before lunch.

Now Marcie glanced at the dashboard. The outside temperature was sixty degrees. When she'd left home, the temperature had been hovering around thirty.

On a whim, Marcie exited the interstate and meandered aimlessly through small Southern towns, enjoying the scenery. She'd never been to the Carolinas before. The word *Carolina* had such a nice ring to it. Now the sound of the word was only a memory.

Marcie squinted into the afternoon sun and noticed a sign for the Magnolia Harbor Inn. She decided to stop and see if there was a room available. She had always wanted to stay in a bed-and-breakfast. She might as well check something off her bucket list. Flipping on her blinker, she waited for two cars to pass and then pulled into the driveway of the elegant inn.

For a moment, Marcie sat in the car with the engine off, admiring the impressive structure. She leaned forward, practically hugging the steering wheel, in an effort to take in the full building. Failing that, she opened her door and stepped outside. The three-story antebellum mansion featured a wraparound veranda on the first and second floors. White columns were positioned at even intervals across the front. The whole place seemed like a vision from another time. A time when life moved at a slower pace.

A warm breeze blew her blonde hair across her face. Absently, she brushed the strands behind her ear. Inhaling deeply, she closed her eyes to savor the richly scented air. The air certainly didn't smell this way back home in Illinois. The warmth of the December day soaked into her skin. It didn't feel this way back home either. Magnolia Harbor, South Carolina, seemed like the ideal place to rest and regain her balance.

Marcie opened her eyes and turned in a slow circle to see the entire area surrounding her. The expansive grounds were meticulously maintained. Old trees towered above her. They had witnessed all the history this house had gone through and still stood tall like unconquerable sentries.

Unconquerable sentries? She shook her head. She was getting a bit fanciful lately, and she needed to be practical now more than ever.

Marcie examined the front of the inn and noticed a holiday wreath on the door. She smiled. It seemed unreal that Christmas was less than two weeks away. She was used to snow and frigid temperatures at this time of year. It was a novel experience to go outdoors in December without bundling up.

Her smile faded as reality sank in. She would have to return to her new life by Christmas. It was not a prospect she relished. Would she still be able to keep her job and practice law? She'd been preparing for this day for a long time, but she'd never thought it would actually come.

Marcie had grown up with a mild hearing loss. It was so mild that it hadn't bothered her. As she'd grown older, her hearing had deteriorated slightly. By the time she was fourteen, she'd suffered a moderate loss in her left ear, so she missed some speech sounds. She'd refused to wear a hearing aid, determined to hide her struggle as much as possible, so she'd been forced to adapt in school. Marcie sat with her good ear toward the rest of the class and watched what the other students were doing. Her teacher of the deaf and hard of hearing called them "coping strategies."

Her audiologist had told her that she'd probably lose all her hearing one day. After the grim diagnosis, her mother had insisted that Marcie learn to read lips. For her entire high school career, Marcie had worked with an itinerant teacher of the deaf and a speech and language pathologist on lipreading and muscle memory to learn how to form words and control her volume.

Although Marcie had been warned, she never truly believed she'd lose her hearing until she'd woken up one morning and it was gone.

Her phone vibrated, startling her out of her thoughts. She pulled it out of her pocket and checked the screen. It was a text from her best friend, Allie. *Checking in to make sure you're okay.*

I'm fine. Arrived at the most adorable B & B. Will send pics later. Marcie hit send.

Allie responded immediately. *When will you be home?*

Marcie frowned, wondering how to answer. Allie knew some of what was bothering her, but Marcie hadn't even told her best friend about all the anxiety and fears that had been swirling around in her mind lately. Talking about it would have made everything seem too real, but holding it in wasn't healthy either. She needed to reply, but she didn't want to have a long discussion via text.

I'm not sure yet. I'll let you know. I have a lot on my mind that I'll tell you about when I get home.

I love you, and I'm praying for you.

Thanks. Love you too. Talk to you soon. Marcie slid the phone back into her pocket. It was silly to stand out here. She needed to go inside and see if they had a room available. She retrieved her purse from the car, then strode to the mansion.

As she climbed the steps, she admired the front porch. The wooden floor was polished to a shine. White wicker rocking chairs invited her to sit down and relax. She would definitely have to take advantage of those while she was here. It would be pleasant to drink her morning tea on this charming porch.

Marcie entered the bed-and-breakfast and paused just inside the foyer, her mouth hanging open. She'd never been inside one of these mansions before. The interior of the inn was exquisite. And she was only seeing the foyer. The ceiling was high, giving her a view of the curved staircase and the railing that wrapped around the second-floor hallway. White walls and a pristine white-and-black patterned floor spread out before her. A beautifully decorated Christmas tree was perfectly placed at one side. Beyond that, she could see through to a large arch into the next area.

A lovely woman stood behind the reception desk. She had wavy dark-brown hair with golden highlights. "Welcome to the Magnolia Harbor Inn. I'm Grace Porter, one of the owners. How may I help you?"

Before Marcie could respond, a little dog bounded around the counter to greet her. He plopped down at her feet and gazed up at her adoringly.

"What a sweetheart," Marcie said as she bent to pet him.

"That's Winston," Grace said. "He loves making new friends."

Marcie studied Winston. He was an unusual mix, and she couldn't place his breed. "What kind of dog is he?"

Grace smiled. "I know he's part shih tzu, but the other part is a mystery."

"Well, he sure is cute." Marcie gave him one final pat, then straightened. She approached the desk and held out a hand to Grace. "It's nice to meet you. I'm Marcie O'Connor. I don't have a reservation, but I'm hoping that you have a room available for the next few days. Maybe a week."

"Yes, we have a room that I'm sure would suit you nicely."

At least that was what Marcie thought she said. She had a slight problem reading her lips, but she was fairly confident that she'd gotten the gist of it.

"So, you own the inn?" Marcie winced as soon as she asked the question. Striking up a conversation was not what she wanted to do right now. She needed to be alone.

"I own it with my sister, Charlotte Wylde," Grace said. "She's an amazing chef, and she's written several best-selling cookbooks."

Marcie shifted her weight. As she moved, she knocked her purse off the counter. It was open, and the contents scattered all over the floor. Mortified, Marcie ducked and quickly collected her belongings and shoved them back into her purse. This wouldn't have happened if she had zipped it like Brian always told her. She forced herself to stop thinking about her ex-fiancé. It would spoil her day, and she'd allowed him to spoil too many days already.

When Marcie finished, she glanced at Grace. The innkeeper seemed perplexed.

Marcie stilled. Grace must have been talking to her, and she was expecting a response. Her soul quailed against the idea of explaining, but it would have to be done so she wouldn't offend the woman by appearing rude. She took a deep breath. "I'm sorry. Did you say something? I'm afraid I didn't hear you. I'm deaf."

She waited for the look of pity to dawn on the other woman's face. After all, that was how her coworkers reacted. Some of them had no idea she knew how to read lips. A few of the comments she'd intercepted after her hearing was gone had been less than kind.

Her pool of trusted friends had dwindled down to Allie.

But the dreaded expression didn't come. "Oh, I didn't realize that," Grace said, apparently taking this in stride. "I'm guessing you can read my lips."

Relieved, Marcie nodded. "Mostly. Some of what you say may get lost, but I can understand the majority."

"Please let me know if you need me to repeat anything." Grace picked up a key. "I'm going to put you in the Bluebell Suite if that's all right. You'll have a partial view of the lake and a soaking tub in the room. You'll share a bathroom with the guest in the next room. She's due to arrive tomorrow."

"That's fine. I just need a few days to unwind and think. This inn seems perfect for that."

"Yes, I believe it's the ideal place to rest and regroup," Grace said with a smile. "I hope you enjoy your stay."

Marcie followed Grace up the stairs to the second floor, conscious of Winston at her heels. The presence of the little dog was comforting. She'd never owned a pet before. Allie had been pushing her to consider getting a service dog, but so far, she'd resisted.

She might need to rethink the idea.

Grace stopped in front of the Bluebell Suite and unlocked the door, allowing Marcie to enter the room first.

Marcie gazed around the suite. It was exquisite. The walls were a lovely robin's-egg blue, and the hardwood floor gleamed. A king-size bed with an impressive headboard dominated the room. At the foot of the bed was a white love seat with a plush blue ottoman. A soaking tub stood against a wall with a white fireplace on the adjacent wall.

Walking to the French doors, Marcie peered out at the veranda. From where she stood, part of the lake was visible. Peace she hadn't felt in weeks seeped in.

A few moments later, she felt Grace's presence at her shoulder. She blinked to clear the sudden tears. She would not cry in front of her hostess.

"Are you all right?" Grace asked, sounding concerned.

How could she answer that? Her life was in turmoil, and her future was vague. She didn't want to lie, so she avoided the question altogether. "This room is wonderful."

Grace nodded, obviously aware that Marcie hadn't answered the question. She didn't press, though.

Marcie appreciated that Grace respected her need for privacy.

"Please join us for hospitality hour this evening at six on the back veranda," Grace said. "If it's too chilly, we'll gather in the dining room. You can meet your fellow guests, and Charlotte is planning some delicious appetizers."

"Great," Marcie said. "I had lunch in my car, and I have some food with me, so I should be good until this evening."

And probably longer. She didn't have the strength to mingle with a group of strangers tonight, not while her heart was still shattered from the past few weeks. Her stomach felt queasy at the mere thought of food.

"Breakfast is served in the dining room, and lunch and dinner are on your own," Grace continued. "There are several nice restaurants in the area."

"Thank you," Marcie said.

Grace handed her the key. "Let me know if you need anything else." She left with Winston on her heels.

Sighing, Marcie stood for a minute in the middle of the room. The complete silence still startled her.

She needed to get used to the quiet. This was her life now, and there was no going back.

3

Grace

Grace left Marcie in her room and returned downstairs. Winston's toenails clicked on the hardwood as he padded alongside her. She'd seen the anguish in the younger woman's eyes. As much as she hated leaving her in distress, Grace knew she needed to allow Marcie time to figure out her situation for herself. Most people weren't comfortable turning to strangers for help. Grace would be available for her if she wanted to talk.

Grace rounded the corner, and Winston brushed against her legs. A man stood at the reception desk, and there were two suitcases at his feet. Beside him was an adorable little girl. She couldn't have been older than five or six. It was easy to see the two were related. They both had the same shade of brown hair.

"Welcome to the Magnolia Harbor Inn," Grace said as she hurried behind the desk. "I'm sorry to keep you waiting. I'm Grace Porter, one of the owners, and you must be Charles Johnston."

"Yes, and this is my daughter, Savannah."

Winston bounded over to the little girl and whined softly.

Savannah's face lit up, and a tiny squeak left her mouth. Excited, she signed to her father.

"I'm assuming the dog is safe to pet?" Charles asked Grace.

"Absolutely. Winston adores children, and he's very friendly."

Charles nodded, then signed something to his daughter.

Savannah's delight was unmistakable. She immediately hugged Winston.

"I think Winston's in love," Grace remarked as she watched the dog enthusiastically wag his tail.

"Savannah has a way with animals," Charles said.

"Let's get you checked in." Grace reviewed Charles's reservation. "I have you staying until this coming Sunday." She handed him a registration form.

"That's correct," Charles said. He signed the form and returned it to her.

"I have you in the Buttercup Suite," Grace continued. "You have a king-size bed, a private bath, and a full view of the lake." There was no mention of a child in the reservation. She hoped she hadn't made an error. "I'm sorry, but I didn't make any special accommodations for your daughter."

"Don't worry about it," Charles said. "I had to bring Savannah along at the last minute. My sister was supposed to watch her, but she fell and broke her ankle."

"I'm sorry about your sister's injury," Grace said.

"Will it be a problem for Savannah to stay here?" Charles asked.

"Of course not," Grace assured him. "I'll bring up a folding cot and extra bedding later."

"I wanted to skip my business meetings and stay home, but it wasn't an option," Charles said. "I had to bring Savannah with me, so I'm not sure what to do when I have to work."

"I might be able to find someone who can solve that problem." Grace had the perfect person in mind. Winnie Bennett was her aunt, and she lived nearby. Winnie stopped by the inn often, and she was warm, with a giving heart and a willingness to help out in any situation.

"That's kind of you to offer," Charles said. "But I couldn't impose."

"It's not an imposition," Grace said. "My aunt Winnie is wonderful, and she's close by. Why don't I connect you two? If you like her, we can try it out. If you're still not comfortable, then no big deal."

"I'd be willing to meet her." Charles glanced at his daughter, who was still petting Winston. "Savannah's a good kid. If it works out, I'm sure she won't cause any problems."

"I'm sure she won't," Grace said. "Let me show you to your room, and then I'll get the cot and see if I can contact my aunt."

Charles picked up the luggage.

Grace led the father and daughter to their room. "Please join us this evening on the back veranda at six. My sister, Charlotte Wylde, is an incredible chef, and she'll be offering delicious appetizers. Breakfast is served in the dining room, and lunch and dinner are on your own."

Charles set their luggage inside the door. "We'll have to go out and get something to eat before hospitality hour. We had a late breakfast and haven't eaten since. Where would you recommend?"

Grace studied him. The poor man looked like he might keel over any moment. "We don't usually offer afternoon snacks, but I can bring you some sandwiches."

Relief flickered across his face and quickly disappeared. He shook his head. "I don't want to put you out."

"Nonsense," she said. "I've made sandwiches for guests before, and I'll do it again. It's Southern hospitality."

Charles hesitated. "Are you sure you don't mind?"

"Not at all," Grace said. She left before he could change his mind.

Within thirty minutes, Grace had installed a cot in his room and delivered a tray with turkey sandwiches, bottled water, and sliced fruit. "Just set the tray outside the door when you're done."

Savannah snatched up a sandwich and started gobbling it down.

"Thank you," Charles said to Grace. "I really appreciate this."

"You're very welcome. Please let me know if you need anything else." She left the room and went downstairs.

The bell above the front door jingled, and Winnie stepped inside. With an excited yip, Winston charged over to greet her.

Laughing, Winnie reached down to pet him. "It's nice to see you too, Winston."

"I didn't hear a car pull up," Grace said. "Did you drive?" Her aunt lived with her husband, Gus, less than a mile from the inn, but she usually stopped by on her walks.

Winnie's bright smile lit up her hazel eyes as she beamed at her niece. "It's such a lovely afternoon, I couldn't resist a walk. I'm only staying for a few minutes. I wanted to check on you and make sure everything was going smoothly."

Grace shook her head, amused. She should have expected it. Winnie always seemed to know when she was needed. "You have impeccable timing. Charles Johnston is here on business. His sitter broke her ankle, and he had to bring his daughter. Savannah is a sweet little girl. I offered to see if you could stay with her while he's at his meetings."

"Oh, the poor man," Winnie said. "I'd be delighted to help. I can't promise that I'll be available at all times, but I'm sure we can work something out."

"I thought I heard your voice." Charlotte breezed into the foyer and gave Winnie a hug.

Winnie patted Charlotte's cheek. "It's been at least a day since I came to visit."

The women chuckled.

"So tell me about the other guests," Winnie said.

"The four people coming for the medical conference are arriving tomorrow," Grace said. "The Smiths had to cancel their reservation, but we had a walk-in take their suite."

"How convenient," Charlotte remarked.

"Marcie O'Connor showed up a little while ago," Grace said. "She seems to be struggling with something."

"I'm sure her stay at the inn will be the respite she needs," Winnie said.

"Marcie's deaf, but she reads lips," Grace added. "Oh, and Savannah is deaf too."

"Thanks for letting us know," Charlotte said. "I'll be sure to face Marcie when I talk to her."

Grace's phone rang. She removed it from her pocket and checked the screen. It was Spencer, and she quickly answered.

"It's been too long since I saw you," Spencer said.

She grinned. "I was telling Charlotte that very thing earlier."

"I'm hoping you're free tomorrow evening."

"Tomorrow evening?" Grace gave Charlotte a questioning look. This was a busy week at the inn, and she didn't know if she had time to get away.

Charlotte nodded, pointing between herself and Winnie.

Grace got the message. "Yes, that works for me," she told him. "What do you have in mind?"

Spencer chuckled. "Oh, I don't want to tell you yet. I have a surprise planned."

"I love surprises," she murmured. "Is there a dress code?"

"You're beautiful no matter what you wear, but I plan to wear a tie," he answered.

So they were going somewhere sort of fancy but not quite black tie. "Good to know. I'm sure I can find something suitable."

"I'm sure you can," Spencer said. "I'll pick you up at eight. Does that work?"

"I'll be ready." When Grace disconnected, she glanced up to see Charlotte and Winnie staring at her expectantly.

"Well?" Charlotte asked, brown eyes gleaming.

"Spencer asked me out tomorrow night," Grace said. "He's wearing a tie, but he wouldn't tell me where we're going. It's a surprise."

"How romantic," Winnie said wistfully. "You'll have such an amazing evening."

A thousand questions spun through her head. Where would they go? What was the surprise? Her heart thumped with excitement.

After Hank's reappearance, Grace had come close to losing Spencer. They had been moving into a deeper relationship, and she'd called a halt, telling him she wasn't ready to be more than friends. Spencer respected her wishes and allowed her space. Only afterward when Spencer's old flame from college came to town did Grace realize that she loved him.

If she'd learned anything from that experience, it was that Spencer was the man she wanted to grow old with. It had taken a long time, but she was finally ready for a future with him at her side.

She was just waiting for him to come to the same conclusion.

Charles

"Are you finished?" Charles signed to his daughter.

Savannah nodded. She'd eaten a turkey sandwich and a few pieces of fruit, and she was still sipping on a bottle of water.

He was grateful. Savannah could be a fussy eater. She was usually reluctant to try new dishes, but she could handle sandwiches.

Charles collected the plates and set them on the tray. He stood and stretched, easing muscles that ached. He'd been sitting too long today. Maybe he and Savannah would go exploring. It was still light outside. They had more than an hour before their hostesses started serving appetizers.

He picked up the tray and took it to the door to leave in the hall. But when he opened the door, Grace was standing there, her hand raised to knock.

She jumped back with a gasp.

"Sorry," Charles said. "I didn't mean to startle you."

"No, don't apologize. I told you to put your tray outside the door. I never said I'd return to chat." Grace reached for the tray. "I'll take that. I wanted to let you know that my aunt said she'd be delighted to stay with Savannah."

He frowned. "I can't agree yet. I haven't met her." Savannah was his life. He couldn't let her go off with a stranger.

"I understand," Grace said. "She doesn't know if she'll be available whenever you need her. If your schedules match, then I'll introduce you two, and you can take it from there. I don't want you to feel pressured to accept her help."

Some of the tension left his shoulders. "That would work."

"Do you have an itinerary or some kind of schedule you could show her?" Grace asked.

"Yes." Leaving the door open, Charles hurried over to his briefcase and removed his tablet. He opened his e-mail and skimmed the subject lines until he found the one he wanted. Clicking on it, he downloaded the schedule onto his device. "Do you have an e-mail I can send it to?"

Grace rattled off her e-mail address.

He quickly sent the schedule. When he saw that the e-mail had successfully sent, he closed his tablet and slid it into his briefcase.

"As soon as I get downstairs, I'll print it out and give it to Winnie." She handed him a card with Winnie's phone number.

"Thanks." Charles accepted the card, then walked over to his bag. He found his stack of business cards and plucked one out, then gave it to Grace. "The work number listed is also my cell phone. Please let her know she can call or text me anytime."

"I'll give it to her," Grace said. "I'm sure you'll be hearing from her soon."

"If it works and she can help even once, that would be wonderful," he said. "I'm meeting several prospective clients this week. It wouldn't be appropriate to show up with a child, but I refuse to leave her behind. She comes first, before any business deal."

Grace raised her eyebrows. "Will you get into trouble with your boss?"

His neck grew warm. "No. Actually, I own the marketing firm, so no one would complain. However, I don't want to lose new opportunities to expand."

"That makes perfect sense," Grace said. "If there's nothing else, I'll let you go."

"Thank you," Charles said.

Grace nodded and left with the tray.

He closed the door.

Savannah was watching him from near the French doors.

"Do you want to go exploring and see what's around here?" Charles signed to her.

Her eyes lit up, and she grinned.

His chest grew tight. Savannah was the center of his life. He didn't want to think of ever trying to live without her. But if Louis and Margaret Hatcher, his in-laws, had their way, that would be exactly what happened.

Pushing away the terrible thought, Charles took a moment to remember his late wife, Joanna. He missed her so much. They had enjoyed a happy marriage until two years ago when she'd lost her battle with cancer, leaving him and Savannah to carry on without her.

It was a warm evening, so they didn't bother with coats. Savannah held his hand as they walked downstairs. Once outside, they took their time exploring the grounds. They passed a large barn that had been converted into some kind of social hall.

"Is that where they keep cows?" Savannah signed, craning her neck to peer inside. When she didn't see any animals, she stuck her bottom lip out in a pout.

"Not for animals," he told her. "I think they have parties there."

"Will we get to go to a party?"

Charles stifled a sigh. He'd distracted her only to fall into another trap. He scrambled to figure out a way to gently explain that they wouldn't be attending any parties. Savannah was usually very even-tempered, but she had a stubborn streak. When she didn't get her way, tears and meltdowns were not uncommon.

Someone called his name.

Charles turned in relief, glad to have an excuse not to answer his daughter's question yet.

Grace walked toward him with Winston.

Savannah bolted past him and ran to Winston. In seconds, she was on the ground beside the dog, petting him and crooning to him.

Charles watched his daughter signing to the dog, telling him, "Good dog." The sweetness of it put a lump in his throat. Joanna would have loved seeing their daughter like this.

"I wanted to see if you and Savannah were interested in joining us for hospitality hour," Grace said.

"That sounds nice," Charles responded. He got Savannah's attention and signed to her.

Grace ushered them to the back veranda, where two women were arranging the food.

Grace gestured to the younger woman. "This is my sister, Charlotte. She's responsible for all the delicious food." She indicated the other woman. "And this is Winnie Bennett, our aunt."

Charles cleared his throat. "It's a pleasure to meet you both."

"I hope you enjoy the appetizers," Charlotte said.

"Grace said you might need someone to babysit your daughter while you're working," Winnie began.

He nodded.

"I've reviewed your itinerary," Winnie continued. "I can watch Savannah while you're in meetings. The day that might be a problem for me is Thursday afternoon because I have an appointment. Otherwise, Savannah is more than welcome to hang out with me at my house, and we can borrow Winston."

"If you don't mind, can we talk for a few minutes?" Charles asked Winnie. Before he allowed her to care for Savannah, he wanted a little more information about her.

"Of course."

The two of them sat down at a table.

"I live less than a mile away with my husband, Gus," Winnie said. "I stop by and see my nieces often."

"That's wonderful," Charles said. "How long have you been married?"

"Gus and I were high school sweethearts," she said. "We've been married more than fifty years."

"That's impressive," he said. "I don't know many people who can boast that. Do you have any children?"

"Four grown daughters," Winnie said.

"Did they run you ragged the way mine does?" he joked. "She's only five, but she can be a handful at times."

Winnie nodded. "I think a little drama is normal with girls."

As they talked, Charles found Winnie to be intelligent, kind, and honest. At the same time, she wasn't shy about voicing her opinions. He liked her immensely, and he immediately trusted her and knew she would take excellent care of Savannah.

By the time Charles and Winnie had rejoined her nieces at the buffet table, he'd agreed to let Winnie watch Savannah for two of the three days. He held in a sigh of satisfaction. Tuesday and Wednesday were covered. It was better than he'd hoped for. He needed to figure out how to handle the final meeting on Thursday, but he still had a few more days to make arrangements.

When Savannah came over, Charles introduced her to the women, giving them name signs so she would know who he was talking about. Name signs were useful. They eliminated the need to finger-spell every name. Plus, if two names were similar, they could easily be distinguished by their unique name signs.

He signed Winnie by tapping the hand shape for *W* against the opposite shoulder. "Winnie said you can stay with her while Daddy goes to his meetings."

Savannah frowned.

"Tell her I have a cat," Winnie suggested.

When he told Savannah, her eyes grew round. "I've never played with a cat before."

"I know," he signed. "Maybe you could play with Winston too."

"Yay!" Savannah exclaimed.

Charles chuckled, then repeated what she had said for the three women.

"Well, I'm glad that Winston made such a good impression," Winnie said, laughing softly. "He loves people."

Charlotte motioned to the food. "Please help yourself."

Charles filled his plate and made one for Savannah. He was glad there were cheese and crackers and pizza bites because he knew she wouldn't touch the crab puffs. He carried the plates to a table, and Savannah sat down beside him.

Three young women walked onto the veranda, and Grace went over to greet them.

A few minutes later, Grace ushered the newcomers over to Charles and Savannah. "I'd like to introduce you to Becky, Denise, and Mary. They're cousins here for a get-together."

"Nice to meet you," Charles said.

"Charles and Savannah arrived earlier today," Grace told the women, then invited them to sit down at a nearby table.

"I can't believe we're leaving tomorrow," Becky said. "I had such an amazing time."

"I hope we can do it again next year," Denise said.

"We'd love to have you," Grace said. "Just let us know when you're coming."

They all continued chatting as they savored the food and the lovely view.

Soon Savannah started yawning. Charles thought that maybe an early night would be good for her.

"Please excuse us," Charles said. "Savannah needs some rest, so we're going to return to our room."

Charles and Savannah said their goodbyes. They walked inside and climbed the stairs to their suite on the second floor.

When Savannah didn't argue about getting ready for bed, he knew she was exhausted.

Charles tucked his daughter into her cot and helped her say her prayers. When she looked up at him, he could see traces of Joanna in her sweet smile and the curve of her cheek. Love for this tiny miracle welled up inside him as he softly kissed her forehead.

He switched off most of the lights so she wouldn't be disturbed, then moved over to the stuffed armchair on the other side of the room to work. A few minutes later, a yawn caught him by surprise. He needed to go to bed soon, but first he wanted to go over one of the proposals he'd received in his e-mail.

Charles was finishing an e-mail when his phone rang. He glanced at the number and scowled. It was Louis, his father-in-law.

He'd gotten along fine with his in-laws when he and Joanna had married, but little by little, he'd seen how controlling Louis and Margaret were. How much Louis had wanted to keep Joanna under his thumb. She'd loved her parents, but she had been ready to have a family of her own.

When Savannah was born, Charles and Joanna had adored her, and they had been devastated to learn that she was profoundly deaf. Charles still winced when he recalled that initial reaction, although the doctors assured him it was normal.

Charles and Joanna had explored every possible option for their baby. When they had come to the conclusion that American Sign

Language was the best choice, both of them attended classes to learn ASL. It was a difficult language to master, but they were determined to communicate with their daughter.

To their joy, Savannah had blossomed. She was bright and happy, and her communication skills advanced at a rapid pace.

However, Louis and Margaret weren't pleased. They insisted that Charles and Joanna should have made an effort to bring Savannah up oral, but Charles thought they should have made an effort to learn sign language. They refused because they found sign language embarrassing.

As much as Charles wanted to ignore the call, he couldn't do it. After all, they were still Joanna's parents. Grimacing, he answered the phone, then closed his eyes and waited.

"Charles." His father-in-law's voice held a slight accusation, even in a simple greeting. "I went by Monica's house this afternoon."

Charles held his temper as acid churned in his stomach. Why would Louis go to Monica's house? The man made no effort to disguise his disdain for Charles's sister. His main issue with her seemed to be that she worked as a social worker, which according to Louis was a dead-end job.

"Did you hear me?" Louis demanded when Charles didn't answer.

"I heard you," Charles said, tightening his jaw. "I don't know why you went there."

"To see my granddaughter."

Charles wanted to remind Louis that her name was Savannah, but he held his tongue. He had never heard his father-in-law call her by name. It was strange how his in-laws seemed overly protective of Savannah, but they made no true efforts to get to know her.

"She's not with Monica," Charles said. "I have her with me."

"So I learned. Why would you take her with you?" The accusation came through loud and clear.

"She's my daughter," Charles replied, wondering why it was any of the man's concern. "She belongs with me."

Louis snorted. "You should have brought her here to Margaret and me. We would have taken her."

Charles had not even considered it. He knew Louis was trying to figure out a way to get Savannah away from him. The man was insane if he thought Charles would let that happen. "I didn't want to bother you," he said. "Anyway, she's fine. We're enjoying a little time alone together."

"I don't think you understand the scope of what you've done," Louis snapped. "You've taken her out of school. What were you thinking?"

"It's preschool," Charles reminded him. "Her teacher said it wouldn't hurt her, and it could actually help her. Give her more background knowledge."

He recalled his conversation with Savannah's teacher. According to her, more experiences would help Savannah understand more concepts, which would enhance her vocabulary and communication. She called it "schema." He trusted her a whole lot more than Louis.

"Background knowledge," Louis repeated, scorn dripping from his voice. "It sounds ridiculous. I have serious doubts about letting you raise that child."

"*Letting* me?" Charles kept his voice low, anger seething inside him. "You forget that she's my daughter. She's happy, healthy, and well cared for. That's all you need to know."

"She might be your daughter," Louis said, his tone icy, "but it doesn't mean that you're fit to raise her. You think about that." He hung up.

Charles felt the threat in the man's words. Louis had finally admitted what Charles had always suspected. He was planning something. No doubt he'd already hired a team of expensive lawyers.

They were going to try and take his daughter away from him.

And as long as he was alive to fight it, they would fail.

Grace

Grace checked the clock on her bedside table and groaned. Five in the morning. She'd been exhausted when she'd finally gone to bed last night, but apparently that wasn't enough to ensure a full night's rest. She'd woken up twice during the night and struggled to get back to sleep. This time, she accepted that she was up for the day.

She knew why she was so restless. She was excited about seeing Spencer tonight. Her mind was whirling with questions about his surprise. Where were they going? Something in his voice had sent her heartbeat racing. Tonight was important—she could feel it in her bones.

Which was why Grace was determined to get everything done. She couldn't cancel her date. But she had a mile-long list of things to do at the inn. She had a medical conference to prepare for. Not to mention the Christmas party on Friday. She wasn't even close to being ready for it.

Throwing back her blankets, Grace swung her legs over the edge of the bed, then slid her feet into her slippers and got up.

Winston rose from his bed and followed her into the kitchen. He made a beeline for his food bowl.

Grace smiled. He probably had no idea how early it was. She normally fed him when she woke in the morning. "An early breakfast it is," she told him. She poured kibble into his bowl and freshened his water.

After starting a pot of coffee, Grace left the dog to his meal and returned to her bedroom for a shower. She selected a pair of black pants and an emerald-green blouse, and she put on a long necklace with beads in various shades of green. She was going to be on her feet most of the day, and she wanted to be comfortable, so she slipped into low-heeled black pumps.

By the time she was ready, Winston had curled up on his dog bed in the bedroom again.

"I don't blame you," Grace said with a laugh.

In the kitchen, she made an omelet and toast. Usually she ate breakfast when the guests did, but she was too hungry to wait. After pouring a cup of coffee, she sat down at the island to eat, leafing through the local newspapers. She liked to be able to tell the guests about events in Magnolia Harbor and nearby towns in case they were interested.

When she was done, she quickly cleaned up and strode to the reception desk, where she responded to the inn's e-mails.

As she checked the calendar, she realized she'd mixed up the dates for the medical conference. She'd thought it started tomorrow morning with the first session, but it was scheduled to begin this evening with the keynote speaker. Fortunately, there was no dinner to prepare, but the barn wasn't ready for guests. She'd have to work fast. A sinking feeling in the pit of her stomach warned her it would not be enough.

Grace grabbed a notepad and a pen, hoping a plan of action would calm her down. She made a list of everything she needed to accomplish today. Besides preparing the barn, she needed to make phone calls, clean the suites for the new arrivals, and take care of the last-minute details for the conference.

She set the pen down and studied the list, feeling even more overwhelmed. How in the world would she be able to finish all these tasks by this evening?

Becky, Denise, and Mary quietly descended the stairs with their luggage. The cousins approached the desk and set their bags on the floor.

Grace folded the to-do list and stuffed it into her pocket. "Are you leaving already?"

"Afraid so," Mary said. "We decided to get an early start."

"I hope you all enjoyed your stay," Grace said, checking the women out.

"It was the most fun I've had in ages," Becky gushed.

"I'm so glad," Grace said. "Since you're missing breakfast, can I get you some coffee and blueberry muffins for the road?"

"That would be great," Denise said.

"I'll be right back." Grace hurried to the kitchen and prepared the snacks. She returned with cups of coffee and muffins and handed them out.

"Thank you," Becky said.

The women promised to return next year, then said goodbye and left.

Grace checked the clock. It was still too early to make any phone calls. She decided to start with the suites. The rooms the cousins had vacated needed to be cleaned for the medical conference attendees.

Grace grabbed her cleaning supplies and went up to the Wisteria Loft Suite on the third floor, careful not to disturb the guests on the second floor. She remembered when Sam Matthews had called to book his room. He'd requested this suite because he liked the idea of staying in a loft. She'd laughed when he said it would make him feel like a kid again. She pictured Sam as a youthful man around thirty with a ready grin. Probably a practical joker. She hoped he liked the room.

As Grace cleaned, she admired the lovely suite. It featured a view of the lake. The king-size bed and antique bedroom set were gorgeous, complete with an ornately carved wooden headboard, a dresser with a mirror, and a bedside table. Two chairs flanked the white fireplace, creating a cozy sitting area.

After making the bed, Grace stocked the private bath with a full supply of linens, soap, and other products, then scanned the room. Satisfied, she gathered her cleaning supplies and headed out of the room. On the way, she checked the clock. It was time to help Charlotte with breakfast. The other two rooms would have to wait.

Grace returned downstairs, stowed the cleaning supplies, and entered the kitchen.

Charlotte glanced up from the island, where she was slicing a quiche, and grinned. "Good morning."

"You seem awfully chipper this morning," Grace remarked. "I take it your date went well last night."

Charlotte smiled. "Yes, it was wonderful. Dean and I had dinner at his house, and then we caught a movie." Her smile faded as she studied her sister's face. "What's wrong? You seem stressed."

"I'm fine. Just a lot to do today." Grace waved her hand dismissively. "Can I help you with breakfast?"

"It's almost ready." Charlotte picked up the pan of quiche and a platter of bacon and sausage. "The coffee is already in the dining room, but you can grab the orange juice."

Grace retrieved the pitcher of juice from the fridge and followed her sister to the dining room. As they arranged the food and drinks on the sideboard, Charlotte kept sneaking peeks at Grace.

She ignored her sister's worried looks and did her best to keep the conversation light and cheerful. Even to her own ears, it sounded off, and she knew Charlotte noticed.

Grace regarded the dining room. It was furnished with a long elegant table and comfortable high-backed chairs. There was a spectacular view of the lake. She and Charlotte usually enjoyed mingling with the guests during breakfast, but today Grace found it hard to keep her mind off her lengthy to-do list.

Charles and Savannah entered the room.

"We're not too early, are we?" Charles asked.

"Not at all," Grace said. "Please come in and help yourself to the buffet. Would you like a cup of coffee?"

"Yes, thank you," Charles said. He ushered his daughter to the sideboard, and they filled their plates. "Would it be all right if we eat on the veranda? We'd like to enjoy the mild weather."

"Of course," Grace answered, handing him a cup of coffee.

Father and daughter took their plates and headed outside.

Grace went to her private quarters to check on Winston. She found him still sleeping in his dog bed.

When he saw her, he yawned and stretched.

"I know what you mean. It's that kind of morning." Grace scratched behind his ears. "Let's see if our guests need anything."

Winston hopped out of bed and followed her to the veranda.

Charles and Savannah were sitting at a table. The little girl waved at Grace as she approached them with Winston on her heels.

When Savannah reached out to pet the dog, her father stopped her with a few signs. She pouted but dutifully returned her attention to her food.

"I told her that she could pet him after she finished her breakfast," Charles explained to Grace. "She tends to have a one-track mind when she sees a dog. I want to make sure she eats."

"I understand. Winston will be more than happy to play with her when she's done."

Charles relayed what she had said to Savannah.

The girl tilted her head as she considered her father's words. Pursing her lips, she signed back to him.

"She says she doesn't like her choices," Charles told Grace. "But she'll finish her breakfast."

Grace smiled. "I think she's a very smart young lady."

Savannah tucked into her food, keeping an eye on Winston the whole time. Obviously, she intended to pet the dog the instant her fork hit the empty plate.

Winston watched her too, his tail wagging furiously.

"Is there anything else I can get you?" Grace asked.

"No thank you," Charles said. "We're fine."

Winnie stepped onto the veranda. She greeted everyone, then pulled out a chair and sat down next to Savannah. Soon Winnie and Charles were engaged in a spirited conversation.

Grace smiled as she watched them talk. Winnie was warm and gracious, and Grace knew she was giving Charles the opportunity to get to know her before he left his daughter in her care.

Of course, Savannah would be fine with Winnie. She had raised four daughters with her husband. All of them were married and had children of their own now. Only their youngest, Paisley, still lived in Magnolia Harbor with her husband and two children. Winnie loved spoiling her grandchildren, and she would certainly enjoy spoiling Savannah.

Grace thought that Charles appeared more relaxed than he had when he'd arrived. He struck her as a man who took his role as a father very seriously. The fact that he felt the need to vet Winnie before he left Savannah in the older woman's care strengthened that opinion.

She also had the feeling that he had some heavy issues weighing on his mind.

Didn't they all?

Grace sighed as her own concerns returned to the forefront of her mind. She walked to the dining room, not really seeing it. Had she been too hasty telling Spencer she was free this evening? She hated to consider calling him to reschedule, especially since he planned something special for them. But what else could she do? She feared she'd never be able to get everything done.

"What's bothering you?"

Grace jumped. She'd been so wrapped up in her thoughts that she hadn't heard Charlotte enter the room. She placed her hand over her pounding heart. "You startled me."

"I'm sorry," Charlotte said, putting her arm around her sister's shoulders. "You seem worried. Are you all right?"

Grace noticed Marcie eating alone at the table. This was not the time to discuss her worries. They needed to tend to their guest. Marcie hadn't attended hospitality hour last evening, and Grace wanted to make sure she felt welcome. "I'll tell you what's going on after breakfast. Have you met Marcie yet?"

"Not yet," Charlotte said. "I was just going to introduce myself."

Grace and Charlotte approached the table.

"Good morning," Grace said to Marcie. "I'd like you to meet my sister, Charlotte Wylde. She's the amazing chef who prepared breakfast."

Marcie smiled and leaned back in her chair. "It's lovely to meet you. Breakfast is delicious."

"I'm glad you like it," Charlotte said. "I hope you're enjoying your stay."

"I certainly am," Marcie replied. "I think I'd be happy to stay here forever."

The women chatted for a few more minutes until Marcie received a text.

"Sorry," Marcie said, activating her phone's screen. "It's my best friend. I need to let her know I'm okay."

Grace and Charlotte left her and headed to the kitchen.

"So what's going on?" Charlotte asked.

"I need your advice," Grace said. She didn't want to hurt Spencer, and she was afraid that she might. She didn't know how she could go out tonight because she was so far behind.

Before Grace could explain, Winnie entered the kitchen.

Grace wanted her aunt's opinion too. These women always had her back, and she had theirs. It was the way it was supposed to be. And she knew that if anyone could help her figure out what to do, it was Charlotte and Winnie.

"Am I interrupting?" Winnie asked, glancing between the sisters.

"Of course not," Grace said. "I was telling Charlotte that I need her advice. I'd like yours too."

"What is it?" Winnie asked.

"I need to cancel my date with Spencer tonight," Grace announced.

"You can't do that," Charlotte said.

"I agree with Charlotte," Winnie said. "If your relationship with Spencer is going to work, he has to know that he's a priority with you."

And there it was, the core of her anxiety. Grace knew that she needed to put Spencer first. He would understand if she couldn't, but she didn't like the message it would send. The inn was a big part of her life, but he had won her heart. She wanted him to know that.

"Why would you even consider canceling?" Charlotte asked.

Grace pulled her to-do list out of her pocket. Spreading it out on the countertop, she used her palm to try and flatten out the creases. "This is the list of all the things I have to do today. I realized this morning that the conference starts tonight with a keynote address. We're not ready. We have rooms to clean, the barn to prepare, calls to make, and all the things to get ready for the medical conference. There's no way everything will get done."

Her stomach churned. Her relationship with Spencer wasn't the only thing she needed to worry about. Her reputation was on the line too.

"We'll do all we can to help," Charlotte said.

Winnie nodded.

"I know, and I appreciate it," Grace said. "But it won't be enough."

Winnie snapped her fingers. "I'll ask if The Busy Bees can help us," she said, referring to the quilting group she belonged to.

Grace frowned. "It's really short notice, and Patty works at the hospital during the day." Patty Duncan was a pediatric physical therapist at the Northshore Medical Center.

Winnie searched her phone contacts. "True. But the others might come. And Patty can always join us when her shift is done. We'll never know if we don't ask."

Grace wouldn't get her hopes up. Not yet.

Winnie called Judith Mason, the leader of the quilting group. "We're in a bit of a bind here at the inn."

Charlotte leaned over to Grace. "You go on with your business. We'll come find you when we know who can help."

Grace gave her a doubtful look.

Charlotte nudged her away. "Go on. I mean it."

Nodding, Grace left the kitchen and began working on her list. Even knowing that her sister and aunt were trying to help, she still felt overwhelmed. Although hope had started to work its way into her anxiety.

She managed to get two more items ticked off her list before her sister found her in the Rosebud Suite, cleaning the room for Alyssa Larson. She was scheduled to arrive soon.

"Good news," Charlotte said, leaning against the doorframe. "Judith, Angel, Patty, and Helen have all agreed to lend a hand. Helen, Angel, and Judith will be here within an hour, and Patty will come after work today."

Grace couldn't believe that the entire group was coming to help. "That's wonderful. We'll have to do something for them to show our appreciation."

"I'll bake them something after the conference is done," Charlotte offered.

"Whatever you make, it'll be amazing. Thanks again for everything." Grace smiled at her sister, feeling overwhelmed with gratitude. She was so fortunate to have such kind and caring family and friends.

The tension she'd been harboring finally eased, and she started to relax. Her special evening with Spencer might come true after all.

Sam

Sam Matthews checked his watch for the third time in ten minutes. Alyssa was running late. As usual.

He had told Alyssa that he would pick her up at nine thirty. It was now ten. He'd even called to tell her he was outside her apartment building. When he'd offered to come up, she had very sternly told him that she was quite capable of carrying her own luggage and that she'd be out in five minutes.

"I should have gone inside to get her," he muttered.

Sam wasn't surprised. He had known Alyssa Larson since they were both in third grade. Back then she was still Alyssa Mook. He hadn't really noticed her until they were in fifth grade. She was pretty with her curly black hair and light-brown eyes, but he hadn't noticed her because of her appearance. At least, that wasn't what had kept his attention. Alyssa was intelligent. Sam was too, but he had to work for his grades while she seemed to sail right through school.

By the time they were in high school, he had a full-blown crush on her. When Alyssa had started dating Derek Larson, Sam realized he had fallen in love with her. He had kept his peace, knowing one didn't go after his best friend's girlfriend. But it was more than that. Derek and Alyssa were meant for each other. They dated all through high school, and they even managed to stay together when they attended different colleges.

Derek had considered going to the same college, but Alyssa talked him out of it. They had different goals. Alyssa dreamed of becoming a doctor, and Derek wanted to become an actuary. They needed schools that fit those goals. Not only that, but Derek had gotten a full football scholarship to a state school. His parents couldn't afford to send him to college. And Alyssa knew that she couldn't find what she needed at the same school.

Sam had gone to the same college as Alyssa. It had been difficult to spend time with her as a friend. But it was obvious she was completely devoted to Derek. So even though it broke his heart, Sam smiled as Derek asked him to be his best man when he married Alyssa.

After the wedding, Sam remained friends with Derek and Alyssa. They had wanted Sam to be happy and tried to set him up several times, but there was no woman who could hold his interest.

Two years ago, tragedy struck. Derek had been killed in a car accident on his way home from work. It had nearly destroyed Alyssa. Sam—loving her, loving Derek—had made a point to be there for her as a friend, nothing more. He knew she'd never see him the same way as she had seen Derek. But that was okay. He could still be her friend.

As time passed, Sam found it harder to remain just her friend. He had hoped he'd fall out of love with Alyssa, but it hadn't happened yet. If anything, his feelings had grown even stronger.

It made things even more difficult because Sam and Alyssa worked in the same hospital, and they saw each other every day. He was afraid he'd unintentionally say something that would give his feelings away.

The apartment doors opened, and he stepped out of his car.

Alyssa exited the building, dragging her rolling suitcase and carrying her laptop bag. There was a third bag dangling from her elbow, and it appeared heavy. She grimaced as her shoulder-length hair got caught in the computer bag's strap.

Rushing forward, Sam grabbed the laptop bag and the rolling suitcase, letting her carry the other bag. He returned to the car, pressing his key fob to open the hatchback door of his SUV. After it rose, he set the bags into the car, then waited for her to put the third bag in. As she got close to him, he caught a whiff of her perfume. Or maybe it was her shampoo. Whatever it was, he decided the subtle floral scent suited her.

"I distinctly remember us agreeing to one bag each," Sam remarked as he lowered the hatchback door.

"I never agreed to that," Alyssa said. "You told me you were bringing one bag. My response was noncommittal."

He chuckled as he walked to the passenger side and opened her door. "You're too much."

She stuck out her tongue at him, then slid into the seat.

Sam grinned as he gently closed the door and rounded the car to his side. He got behind the wheel and started the car.

He didn't say anything until they were almost out of Atlanta. "It's a good thing we decided to drive. You would have paid extra to fly with that much stuff."

"We'll be gone for almost a week. That's a lot of outfits." Alyssa shrugged. "Besides, I need to have options."

"Why didn't I think of that?" Sam teased. He glanced at her, prepared to make another wry comment, but the words got stuck in his throat as he watched her smooth her hair away from her face. His gaze was drawn to her left hand. For a moment, he forgot everything.

Whatever comment he'd been planning to say no longer mattered. All that mattered was that the woman he'd loved for the past seventeen years was sitting beside him. He'd felt comfortable while Alyssa was a grieving widow. But now she had removed her wedding rings. She'd worn them every day since Derek had died.

Sam had overheard one of the nurses at the hospital ask Alyssa when she planned to start dating again.

"In my heart, I'm still a married woman." Alyssa had held up her left hand. "Until I feel ready to move on, these rings will remain where they are."

That was nearly a month ago.

Sam hadn't rushed Alyssa to get over her grieving. He'd long ago decided that she was too good for him. The idea of asking her out when she was ready to date again had never occurred to him. Although the idea of her with someone else wounded him.

But now, tension danced across his shoulders at the clear sign that she was ready to move on. His hands tightened on the wheel. Could he ask out his best friend's widow?

What if she said no?

Sam had gotten used to spending time with Alyssa, and he didn't want to risk that. Even if he had to love her from afar, he still had the privilege of being her friend. If he confessed his feelings, it might destroy that bond. Then he'd be denied even the small joys of meeting her for coffee and going to the movies together.

He couldn't imagine his life without her in it.

"What's wrong?" Alyssa asked.

"Nothing," Sam said. He couldn't admit out loud what he'd been thinking. "This is my serious face."

"You could have fooled me," she said. "I thought you were ready to cry."

"I was thinking, but it was nothing morose or sad. Just letting my mind wander."

Her expression said she didn't believe him, but she changed the subject.

They talked about their jobs at the hospital and the medical conference they were going to attend in Magnolia Harbor.

For the rest of the journey, Sam deliberately kept the conversation rolling. He didn't want her getting wind of his mood and asking more questions.

The last thing he wanted to do was lie to her.

Grace

Grace was relieved when the troops showed up. As promised, Judith arrived with Angel Diaz and Helen Daley, and they all appeared ready and willing to work.

Winston bounded into the foyer and raced around in circles.

"You're so adorable," Angel said, scooping up the dog and hugging him. She was the youngest member of the quilting group. A talented artist, she also worked part-time at the Dragonfly Coffee Shop in Magnolia Harbor.

Winston wriggled in Angel's arms.

"I know I'm not the only one you're excited to see," Angel said, gently setting him on the floor.

The dog trotted over to Judith and whined.

"You poor thing. You clearly don't get enough attention." The outgoing leader of The Busy Bees laughed and leaned down to pet him. Judith owned Spool & Thread, a fabric shop in town, where the quilting group met every week.

Winston finally made his rounds to the third member of the group. Helen was the wife of the police captain. She had rheumatoid arthritis, but she didn't let it slow her down.

"Thank you for helping us out," Grace told them. "I can't express how much it means to me."

"It's our pleasure," Helen said. "Besides, you'd help us in a heartbeat."

The others chorused agreement.

Humbled and truly touched, Grace thanked them again.

Charlotte and Winnie joined the group and greeted their friends. Grace took a few minutes to explain what needed to be done.

Judith and Angel headed out to the barn with Winnie, Charlotte went to the kitchen, and Helen tackled the list of phone calls that needed to be made, leaving Grace to get the rooms and accommodations in the inn itself prepared.

As Grace hurried upstairs to the Dogwood Suite, her heart felt much lighter.

They might make it.

Grace cleaned the room in record time. As she scrutinized her work, she couldn't help but admire the beautiful suite. The spacious room offered a full lake view, a four-poster bed, a charming desk, and a fireplace. It was the ideal place to relax.

When she went downstairs, the bell above the front door jingled, and a man and a woman in their fifties entered the lobby. The man carried two suitcases.

"Welcome to the Magnolia Harbor Inn. I'm Grace Porter, one of the owners. You must be Howard and Wanda Reeves." She wanted to let out a sigh of relief. She'd finished cleaning their suite just in time.

"Yes, we are." Howard smiled. "We're glad to finally be here. It was a long drive."

"Let's get you checked in, so you can settle into your room." Grace rounded the reception desk and retrieved a registration form. "Where do you live?"

Howard approached the desk and set the suitcases on the floor. "Nashville." He grinned. "In case you're wondering, no, I'm not a frustrated country singer."

Grace laughed as she slid the form across the counter. She immediately liked Howard. He was cheerful and outgoing, but Wanda acted aloof. She stood awkwardly beside her husband and didn't join the conversation. Grace assumed she seemed a little distant because she was an introvert.

Howard signed the form and returned it to Grace.

"Whenever you're ready, I'll show you to your room," Grace offered.

Wanda sniffed.

Her husband appeared worried, but he remained silent.

Winston bounded into the room and made a beeline for the couple.

"That's Winston," Grace said with a smile. "He loves making new friends."

Wanda's aloof expression changed to one of horror, and she pointed at Winston. "Keep that mutt away from me."

Winston whined and hid behind the reception desk.

"I'm so sorry," Grace said. "He won't hurt you."

Wanda glared at Grace. "That's not the point. I don't wish to be mauled by some dog when I'm at a business conference."

"It's okay," Howard murmured, putting his arm around Wanda's shoulders. "He didn't touch you. Let's go to our room and relax. You'll feel better after you rest."

Grace grabbed the key and ushered them upstairs to the Dogwood Suite.

As soon as Wanda entered the room, she announced, "It's too bright in here." She walked to the windows and closed the curtains, then frowned. "I don't care for the way the furniture is arranged. The bed should be on the other wall."

Grace could tell Howard felt bad about his wife's reactions.

"Why are we staying at this place?" Wanda motioned to the French doors leading out to the veranda. "What if someone breaks in while we're sleeping?"

"We don't need to worry about anything like that," Howard assured her. His gentle tone seemed to calm her down. "We're not in the city anymore. Things are different here."

"Breakfast is served in the dining room," Grace said, changing the subject, "and the medical conference will be providing catered lunches and dinners."

Howard nodded.

"Please join us this evening at six for hospitality hour on the back veranda," Grace continued. "My sister, Charlotte Wylde, is a terrific chef, and she's preparing some delicious appetizers."

"That sounds great," Howard said brightly. "We'll be happy to attend."

Wanda sniffed again.

Howard smiled apologetically at Grace.

She returned his smile to show she understood. Her face felt stiff, and she feared it looked more like a grimace. It wasn't like her to be so off-kilter and impatient. She didn't like it.

"Please let me know if you need anything. I'll let you both get settled in." Grace set the key on the dresser and left the room.

When she arrived downstairs, Winston trotted over to her and whined.

Grace picked him up and cuddled him. "It's not your fault that Wanda was upset. She must be tired from her long trip."

At least she hoped that was the case. Otherwise, it might be a long week.

8

Sam

Sam spotted the sign for the Magnolia Harbor Inn and went down the long drive lined with trees and shrubs.

Alyssa opened her window. "Isn't this heavenly? I could cheerfully smell this air every day of my life."

Sam rolled down his window. He had to admit she was right about the scents floating in the breeze. "It's a lot different than the city."

"So true."

He parked the vehicle, and they got out.

When they went to gather their luggage, Sam reached for two of her bags.

"You don't have to do that," Alyssa protested. "I can carry my own luggage."

"Please let me," he said. "You have no idea how the other guys will harass me if it gets out that I carried one bag, and you lugged in three. Have pity on me."

She laughed. "Have it your way. I'd hate to ruin your reputation."

Without thinking, Sam threw her a flirtatious wink. "Thanks for looking out for me."

Her expression grew thoughtful.

He wondered what she was thinking, then shrugged. She'd tell him if she wanted him to know what was on her mind.

They climbed the steps to the front porch, and Sam opened the door.

A bell above the door jingled, and a little dog trotted over to them, wagging his tail in a friendly way.

Alyssa laughed. "What a sweetheart."

"I see you've met Winston," a brown-haired woman said from behind the reception desk. "He loves to welcome our guests."

"He's adorable," Alyssa said.

"He certainly is." The woman smiled. "Welcome to the Magnolia Harbor Inn. I'm Grace Porter, one of the owners. You must be here for the medical conference."

They approached the desk and set their luggage down.

"Yes. I'm Sam Matthews, and this is Alyssa Larson."

"Let's get you checked in," Grace said. She handed them both registration forms, then addressed Sam. "As requested, I have you in the Wisteria Loft Suite."

"Thanks," he said, signing the form and passing it to his hostess.

"You're in the Rosebud Suite," Grace told Alyssa. "It has a garden view, a fireplace, and a queen-size bed. There's a private soaking tub in the room, but you'll be sharing a bathroom."

"That's not a problem," Alyssa said as she returned the signed form to Grace.

"As you know, the medical conference is offering catered lunches and dinners," Grace said. "Please join us on the back veranda for hospitality hour at six. It would be a great time to meet the other guests, and my sister, Charlotte Wylde, is planning some tantalizing hors d'oeuvres. We also serve breakfast in the dining room."

He checked his watch. Hospitality hour was a long time away, and he was already hungry. "Are there any restaurants around here?"

"There are several great options." Grace gave them a map of Magnolia Harbor and pointed out a few places.

"Thanks," Sam said as he stuffed the map into his pocket.

Grace grabbed two keys. "I can show you to your rooms if you're ready."

Sam and Alyssa picked up their bags and followed Grace to the second floor.

Alyssa seemed thrilled with the Rosebud Suite. "I never want to leave."

"Do you want to go into town after you get settled?" Sam asked. "I'll stop by in thirty minutes."

"Sounds great," Alyssa said.

Grace gave Alyssa her room key, then escorted Sam to his suite on the third floor. "It's the only room on this floor, so it's very private."

Sam was impressed with the elegant room that featured a king-size bed with an ornate headboard, a fireplace, and a beautiful view of Lake Haven. This certainly wasn't what he'd expected when he'd requested the loft.

"I hope you enjoy your stay," Grace said, giving him the room key. "Please let me know if you need anything else." She left the room.

He walked onto the veranda and gazed at the lake for a few minutes. A sense of calm settled over him, and his worries faded from his mind. Then he took the map of Magnolia Harbor out of his pocket and studied it. He found several area attractions that sounded interesting.

Soon it was time to go, and Sam jogged down to the second floor. He knocked twice on Alyssa's door and waited.

"I'm coming," she called. "Hold on."

He grinned. He'd told her he'd be back in thirty minutes. It was closer to thirty-five. She was never ready on time for anything except work. She probably told herself she needed to arrive half an hour early for each shift.

Alyssa finally opened the door. Her hair was in a messy bun, and she wore jeans, a long-sleeved pink top, and sneakers. "Sorry I'm late, but I got distracted."

Sam wasn't surprised. Alyssa was always focused at work, but when she wasn't on the job, her thoughts seemed to run in a hundred different directions. "Don't worry about it. Do you have your room key?"

"Right." She dashed over to the nightstand, snatched the key, and returned to the door. "I'm ready."

They walked side by side down the hall.

"I was checking out the map Grace gave us," he remarked as they descended the stairs. "I don't know how much we'll be able to see on this trip. I'd like to come back for a real vacation when I'm not busy."

Alyssa cocked an eyebrow at him. "When are you not busy?"

"Good point. But I'm thinking that I need to take some time to enjoy life. I'll be thirty-two soon. I want to have some fun."

She nodded. "I've been thinking about something similar. I'll never forget Derek, but I have been wondering if it's time I begin to live again. Maybe even date."

His heart and his feet stumbled. "Really?"

"Do you think it's too soon?"

"I don't. Derek adored you, and he'd want you to be happy." *And so do I, even if it's never with me.*

"I'm glad you think so," Alyssa said. "I've been worried. But you're my best friend in the world, so I knew you'd tell me the truth."

His joy dimmed a bit. How could he change from best friend to love interest? Who was he kidding? He didn't have a chance.

Or he wouldn't if he didn't take one.

Sam needed to carefully consider what to do. Now was not the time to declare his feelings for Alyssa. Squaring his shoulders, he focused on giving her a fun afternoon out—no pressure for it to be anything more.

Alyssa stopped in the foyer. "Do we have time to sightsee before the keynote speaker?"

"I think so." He opened the front door, then motioned for her to precede him outside into the sunshine. "If we eat in town, we probably won't be hungry enough to attend the hospitality hour Grace told us about."

They jumped into his car and made the short drive to town. Sam parked, and they strolled around the cobblestone streets. They window-shopped, talking and laughing with the ease of longtime friends. Alyssa admired the Christmas decorations in the windows. He knew she loved all things Christmas. Every year, she went all out, decorating her whole house and sending cards.

Soon he heard her stomach growl. "I believe we need to find a place to eat," he teased.

Her cheeks were flushed. "I should say I'm not hungry, but you'd know that's a lie."

"Why should you?" Sam asked. "We never lie to each to other. It's the code." He cringed as soon as the words left his mouth. It sounded ridiculous.

Alyssa smirked. "Since when do we have a code?"

"Okay, I'm making that up, but I'm hungry too." He took out the map and scanned it. "We could try Aunt Patsy's Porch. It's outside of town on I-95."

She pointed to the map. "Or we could try Why Thai. It's on Main Street, so it's really close."

"I've never tried Thai before. Have you?"

"Once. It was good."

Sam folded the map. "Then Why Thai it is."

They found the restaurant with no problem, and they were seated immediately. Sam ordered the chicken satay skewers, and Alyssa chose the vegetarian Asian stir-fry.

"Are you vegetarian now?" Sam asked. It had been a while since they'd eaten together, but she hadn't been before.

"No, but when we walked in, I heard some ladies raving about it. So I thought I might as well try it. Although the skewers sound good too."

"Do you want to share so we can both try each of them?" he asked.

"Good idea."

The skewers and the stir-fry could have been the tastiest dishes ever, but Sam barely tasted either because he was so focused on Alyssa. He knew it wasn't a date, but it sure felt like one.

As they were leaving the restaurant, Alyssa appeared contemplative again.

"Deep thoughts?" Sam asked.

She laughed slightly. "Not really. I was just thinking about what you said earlier. About us having a code of never lying to each other."

He groaned. "I knew it was a ridiculous remark the minute I said it."

"No." Alyssa put her hand on his arm, stopping him. "It's not. I like it. And I realized that we really do have some sort of code. We've been friends for a long time, and I can't think of anyone I trust more. I like the idea of us having a code, one that says we're always honest with each other."

Sam agreed. He'd never been dishonest with her and never would. Except about how much he loved her.

Marcie

Marcie strolled down the charming Main Street in Magnolia Harbor. As she walked by the Dragonfly Coffee Shop, the tantalizing aromas of coffee and sweet pastries reached out and pulled her in. She entered the shop before she'd made a conscious decision.

The man behind the counter said something to her, but she was too far away to see it.

Marcie approached the counter. "I'm sorry. I'm deaf, and I couldn't read your lips. Could you please repeat what you said?" She was getting tired of having to tell people she was deaf. Even though she'd been hard of hearing most of her life, she usually caught enough of what was happening that she didn't need to ask people to repeat themselves.

The man took care to face her and smiled. "No problem. I said good afternoon. I'm Josh Ford. This is my place."

"Nice to meet you. I'm Marcie." She peered at the pastries displayed in a glass case. "I was walking by, and your shop smelled so enticing that I stopped to see what you had. But everything looks delicious, and I'm having trouble choosing."

She appreciated that he waited to respond until she focused on him. Many people had trouble remembering that she needed to see their mouths to understand them.

"I'm happy to help you find something," Josh said. "Are you a coffee drinker? Or do you prefer tea?"

"I drink both, but I don't experiment much with different flavors or varieties."

"So, something like a medium roast coffee? Or maybe green tea?"

Marcie considered the options. Suddenly, she was bored of always taking the safe route. "I want to challenge my taste buds. Something cold and sweet. I don't care about calories. Not today."

"Oh, living dangerously," Josh said with a grin. "Let's see. Something in the tea family?"

She pressed her lips together. "Something more like coffee. But not with a heavy coffee taste."

Josh described several drinks, and Marcie ended up with a latte macchiato. She paired it with a huge salted caramel muffin.

After paying for her purchases and thanking Josh, Marcie savored her treats at a table in the corner. She had a healthy appetite, but she barely finished the muffin.

As Marcie walked back to her car, she felt full and slightly uncomfortable. It had been worth it, though. She never indulged. After what she'd been through the past few weeks, she'd earned the right to enjoy herself without feeling guilty. Plus, she'd lost eight pounds. Her clothes were starting to get baggy on her.

Back at the inn, she snapped several photos of the beautiful mansion for Allie. Then she returned to her suite and took more pictures. Marcie sat down on the bed and texted Allie the photos.

Allie texted back immediately, wanting an update on her trip.

Marcie told her about the bed-and-breakfast and her excursion to town, then smiled as Allie filled her in on what was happening at home.

After catching up with her best friend, Marcie stretched out on the bed, trying to talk herself into going to hospitality hour. She wasn't hungry. She didn't know anyone. Part of her wanted to lounge in bed with her e-reader. She'd downloaded several new books that she had been waiting to read.

But Marcie was becoming tired of her own company. If she stayed in her room, she'd start feeling sorry for herself. That wouldn't solve anything. She needed to get out and work on improving her lipreading skills. They were very good now, but she still missed things. Even this afternoon, she'd had to ask Josh to repeat himself twice while he was explaining the different kinds of coffee drinks. She should also become more comfortable letting people know what she needed. The itinerant teacher who had worked with her in high school would have called it "increasing her self-advocacy skills."

With a groan, Marcie heaved herself off the bed and took a quick shower to refresh herself. She dressed in a pair of jeans and a blue top with lace details on the shoulders. A light floral cardigan added some flair, and it would keep her from getting too chilly in the evening air. She brushed her blonde hair, leaving it loose to float around her shoulders. She didn't have time to completely redo her makeup, so she brushed mascara on her lashes and put on a light coat of her favorite plum lipstick.

Finally, she slid into strappy sandals with low heels. As a general rule, Marcie avoided high heels. She had inner ear issues, so walking on heels made her feel like she was on a ship in turbulent waters.

Marcie left the room and locked the door behind her. She was the first guest on the veranda, and she helped herself to a few appetizers and a glass of wine. She sipped it slowly as she made her way to one of the tables.

She sat down as close to the lake as she could. The view was spectacular. Bodies of water soothed her soul. If she ever built a house, she wanted it to be near water. Her seat had another advantage. She could see people coming in and out without appearing to be watching them. She felt like a spy, but it was necessary for her survival. She had to learn how to accept her new identity.

Grace and Charlotte walked onto the veranda, carrying two more plates of appetizers. After the sisters set the food down, they headed toward Marcie's table.

Marcie put her glass down and smiled.

"It's nice to see you," Grace said. "I'm so glad you could join us."

"The view is breathtaking," Marcie said, then motioned to her plate. "And everything is delicious."

"I'm happy you think so," Charlotte said. "I still have some things to handle in the kitchen, but please let me know if you need anything." She hustled back inside.

Grace stayed with Marcie. "Are you doing all right?"

"Yes, I am. I—" Marcie broke off and stared as a man in his midthirties stepped onto the veranda with an adorable little girl at his side. They were signing to each other.

Marcie couldn't tell if they were both deaf, but the fluency of the signs took her breath away, even as the man juggled filling plates for himself and his daughter. Signing was something she had never learned. It had never occurred to her as a possibility because she'd never genuinely believed she'd lose all her hearing.

Tears threatened to spill down her cheeks. She wasn't alone. All her life, she'd been the only person at school and work with a hearing loss. So it was overwhelming to see another deaf person at a bed-and-breakfast in a small town in South Carolina.

"They're deaf?" Marcie asked Grace.

The man glanced at Marcie and frowned.

Marcie cringed. She hadn't meant to be so loud.

"Please join us." Grace waved them over.

The man continued to frown as he ushered the girl over to the table.

Marcie fought the urge to sink lower in her seat. This was a mistake. She should have stayed in her room.

"Charles," Grace said, keeping her face toward Marcie, "I want to introduce you and your daughter to Marcie O'Connor."

Charles turned away slightly and said something.

Marcie didn't catch it, but she doubted it was welcoming. He probably thought she was being impolite when she asked if they were both deaf. Well, here was an opportunity to "self-advocate."

"I'm sorry, but I need to see your lips when you talk," Marcie told Charles. "I'm deaf."

His frown melted away, and understanding dawned in his brown eyes. "I can do that." He signed something to his daughter.

The girl smiled and signed back, then motioned to Marcie.

"My daughter wants to know if you are full-deaf like her," Charles said to Marcie. "She has a bilateral profound loss."

Which meant that she was deaf in both ears. Most people didn't realize that there were ranges of hearing loss. Sometimes hearing aids helped, but sometimes they didn't. The little girl wasn't wearing hearing aids. Marcie felt it would be rude to ask why. Maybe she was like Marcie. Hearing aids hadn't helped her at all.

"Yes, I am," Marcie replied, "but I don't know sign language."

Charles signed her answer to his daughter.

A couple walked onto the veranda, and Grace excused herself to greet them.

"Would you sit with me?" Marcie asked. Her cheeks grew warm. "I'm sorry. I don't mean to bug you."

Charles pulled out a chair for himself and another for his daughter. They sat down across from Marcie at the table.

"I didn't catch your name," Marcie said to the little girl. She knew enough to know that one should address the deaf person directly and let the person interpreting take care of getting the message across.

Charles signed her question.

The girl made a gesture with her fisted hand, sliding it down her right cheek.

"That's the name sign for Savannah," Charles explained.

"What a pretty name," Marcie said with a smile.

Savannah pointed at her.

"She wants to know if you have a name sign," Charles said.

Marcie shook her head.

Savannah appeared confused and signed something to her father.

"She wants to know why not," Charles said.

Marcie hesitated. "I haven't been deaf for very long. I was hard of hearing most of my life, so I can lipread pretty well, but I don't know any signs. I lost my remaining hearing suddenly."

She could tell he was curious, but he didn't ask her to elaborate.

Marcie was grateful. She didn't feel like rehashing the drama of the past few weeks to a stranger. Although he had a solid air about him, and Marcie had a feeling that he was someone she could trust. Then again, she'd thought the same thing about Brian, so her judgment was not always reliable.

Grace approached the table with the young couple who had recently arrived. "I'd like you to meet Sam Matthews and Alyssa Larson. They're doctors here for a medical conference."

Marcie was surprised that they weren't married because they seemed so comfortable with each other. She noticed that they didn't wear wedding rings. She was curious, but she didn't want to pry.

"You'll be sharing a bathroom," Grace said to Marcie and Alyssa. "I'm sure you can figure out a schedule."

"I promise not to hog the bathroom," Alyssa joked.

Marcie laughed. "It doesn't matter to me. I'm on vacation, so I don't have anywhere to be. Take as long as you want."

Then Grace introduced Marcie, Charles, and Savannah.

As the group made small talk, an older couple stopped by the table.

"I'm glad to see you two," Grace said to the newcomers. She smiled at the rest of the group. "Please welcome Howard Reeves and his wife, Wanda. They're also doctors here for the medical conference."

Howard greeted the other guests and shook their hands, but Wanda stood farther away and didn't say anything.

Marcie thought that Wanda seemed a little lost.

After a pleasant chat, Grace and the doctors excused themselves.

Alyssa flashed Marcie a smile. "I'll see you around."

Marcie returned the smile. They were nice, and she was happy to have met them. Right now, however, she was more anxious to talk with Charles and Savannah.

Their conversation was halting at times. Charles managed to keep it going between signing for Savannah and remembering to face Marcie so she could read his lips. She appreciated his efforts. And she was amazed that neither he nor Savannah seemed to get frustrated with her blunders and lack of speed.

At one point, Savannah asked if she'd like to learn a few signs.

"Sure," Marcie replied.

Savannah held her open hand in an upright position and touched her forehead with her thumb. That was the sign for dad.

Marcie copied it, feeling silly. She hoped she was doing it right.

The little girl repeated the process for other basic signs.

Marcie didn't have problems with any of them. Savannah made the signs so simple, so beautiful. Marcie wasn't sure if she could ever be comfortable using sign language to communicate, not as well as Savannah and Charles did, but she loved watching the fluid motions the other two made. It was like a dance.

Savannah held up both hands, almost positioned in fists except the index fingers were kept out. She bent the fingers, hooked them together, right over left, before releasing and hooking them again, left over right.

"That's the sign for friend," Charles told Marcie.

Her throat was tight. Marcie certainly needed a friend right now. She repeated the sign and smiled at Savannah, trying to keep her lips from trembling.

They continued talking, and Charles told her that he was here on business and had a meeting tomorrow afternoon. Marcie mentioned she was from Naperville, Illinois.

Charles smiled. "I know that town. I have a client there. We're from Elkhart, Indiana. Only about two and a half hours away from you."

Charles's phone chimed, and he checked the screen. As he read the text, his eyes hardened. He didn't respond to the message. Instead, he switched off his phone and slid it into his pocket.

The beautiful mood that had settled over the three of them was suddenly broken. Charles was distracted, and Marcie could tell that whoever had sent the text had rattled him. She didn't know him well enough to ask him what was going on.

Marcie stood. "I've enjoyed talking with you tonight. Savannah, thank you for teaching me some signs. I'm going to return to my room now."

Charles and Savannah got up to leave as well. Savannah wanted to walk around outside before bed.

Marcie waved at them, then headed to her lonely room. If she'd known them better, maybe they would have invited her along, but she had no intention of getting attached to either the father or the daughter. This inn was a magical place, but she must not forget that it was a brief escape.

She practiced the signs that Savannah had taught her over and over. She hadn't learned enough to hold a conversation, but she didn't want to forget what she had already learned.

Marcie couldn't help but wonder what had upset Charles so much. It had clearly been bad news.

As she recalled his bleak look, she had a horrible thought.

Was something the matter with his sweet daughter?

10

Grace

Grace left the veranda and headed to the barn. Thank goodness The Busy Bees had come to help. She'd been able to complete nearly every item on her list. The caterers from Edible Delights had arrived and set up their tables in the barn. They weren't serving dinner tonight, but they would serve lunch, dinner, and a variety of snacks and drinks for the next few days.

She slipped into the barn to help seat the guests. She arrived before the guests who were staying at the inn and made sure the keynote speaker, an expert in the field of cancer research, had everything she needed.

The guests started to file in, and many of them seemed to know one another. When Howard and Wanda arrived, Grace watched their interactions with the other attendees. Howard appeared well-liked. He was greeted with a lot of back slapping and loud laughter.

His wife was another story. No one approached Wanda. When she joined a group, the others seemed to tolerate her presence, but the conversation became strained. Grace noticed several of the doctors giving her pitying glances before they turned away. It wasn't long before Wanda's scolding voice was the only one heard in the group.

Howard frequently left a group to move to hers, drawing his wife away with some excuse or another, such as he needed her to meet someone or he wanted her opinion. As they left the group, the others watched. A heavy sorrow seemed to follow in Wanda's wake.

Grace was sure something was wrong. At first, she'd assumed that Howard was embarrassed by his wife, but now she could tell that he wasn't. His care for Wanda was exemplary. He cherished her, letting her have some freedom, but he was always mindful of where she was. When she got into trouble, he gently guided her away.

As if she were a child.

Or an adult dealing with early onset Alzheimer's disease.

Suddenly, Wanda's reactions in the inn earlier and her behavior now made much more sense. Grace didn't have any way of knowing if she was correct, but her intuition told her that she was close to the truth.

Wanda was suffering, and her husband was doing his best to help her navigate this new world. That was why the other attendees tolerated her behavior, even though Wanda had clearly made some offensive comments this evening. They were medical professionals, so they knew the signs and were aware that one of their own was deteriorating right in front of them.

"I'm here," Charlotte said. "You can go."

Grace checked her watch. It was nearly time for Spencer to pick her up. Shaking off her sadness, she thanked Charlotte and hurried to the inn. She needed to get ready for her date.

In her private quarters, Winston watched her from his bed as she quickly dressed and reapplied her makeup. Unsure of how dressy she should get, she settled for a little black dress, knowing that it would be appropriate for nearly anything.

She couldn't wait to see Spencer. Her stomach wouldn't settle down, and nervous energy hummed across her skin.

Despite her late start getting ready, she was waiting in the foyer for him ten minutes before he was supposed to arrive.

Spencer walked in at exactly eight, and her breath caught in her throat. He was a man who commanded attention, but he also radiated kindness. He was slightly over six feet tall, and he kept himself in good shape. He had striking light-blue eyes and short salt-and-pepper hair.

When Spencer saw her, his smile lit up his whole face. "You're beautiful as always." He walked over and kissed her lightly.

Grace's lips tingled. It felt like she could finally take a deep breath. "Thank you."

"Are you ready?" he asked.

She nodded.

Spencer escorted her to his black Infiniti sedan that was waiting outside.

Once they were settled inside, Grace asked, "So, where are we going?"

He grinned. "You'll have to wait a little longer to find out."

As they drove, they caught up on each other's lives.

"I had a busy day," Grace said. "I got the event times mixed up for the medical conference, so Winnie and The Busy Bees came to help. It all worked out, but it was a bit tense for a while."

Spencer frowned. "I hate to see you stressed. Should we have rescheduled? We could have tried tomorrow."

His thoughtfulness was one of the many reasons she loved him. It was also why she hadn't rescheduled. "No, I couldn't have done that."

"Why not? I would have understood."

"We both have commitments and people who depend on us for something. There's always going to be something or someone needing our time." Grace lowered her voice. She hesitated to say what was in her heart, but she forced herself to continue. "I decided that if we're going to build a successful relationship, then we have to be a priority for each other. And that's why I couldn't cancel on you."

"I couldn't agree more," Spencer said. "You are definitely a priority with me too."

Grace smiled.

Spencer merged onto I-95 and drove away from Magnolia Harbor. Soon they arrived at a brand-new hibachi restaurant. They'd both been talking about it since they heard about it.

"I didn't realize it was open," Grace said. "What a wonderful surprise."

"It opened last weekend." Spencer parked the car, then opened the door for her and offered his arm.

Grace took his arm, appreciating his old-fashioned manners. Spencer always made her feel special. When she remembered how close she had come to losing him, her heart filled with gratitude.

"Have you been here yet?" she asked as they walked to the door. His daughters, Kylie and Megan, both lived an hour away in Charleston, South Carolina. It wouldn't have been out of character for him to meet them somewhere in the middle for a meal.

"No," Spencer said. "I knew you were anxious to come here, and I wanted to experience it with you."

"I can't wait," Grace said. "I've never been to a hibachi restaurant."

They reached the door, and he opened it for her, allowing her to enter first. As she passed him, he gently placed a hand on the small of her back.

"I was at one years ago," Spencer said.

"How was it?" Grace asked.

"Incredible," he said. "I went with some of my FBI colleagues while we were on a case together. The food was delicious, and the chef was superb. I'm still astonished when I remember his skill."

The young hostess warmly greeted them. Spencer had a reservation, so the woman immediately ushered them to a table and gave them menus.

Grace scanned the menu. "I don't know what to order. Everything sounds fantastic."

Their server came and took their orders. Grace settled on chicken and fried rice, and Spencer ordered steak and fried rice. Both of them asked for glasses of tea.

Their chef arrived and introduced himself. When he started cooking the meat, vegetables, and rice on the grill in front of them, Grace understood what Spencer had meant. The chef deftly chopped, diced, and even tossed food into the air, spearing it as it came back down. He was quick, and he kept up a witty conversation that made Grace and Spencer laugh. When their food was cooked, he bowed and left them to eat in privacy.

"You were right," Grace remarked as she sampled her dish. "The chef was incredible, and the food is delicious. I can't wait to tell Charlotte about this."

"I'm surprised that Charlotte and Dean haven't been here yet," Spencer said, taking a bite.

"They've both been too busy to get away," she said.

They enjoyed their meals for a few minutes, exchanging bites and observations about the food.

"You never did finish telling me about your day," he commented, breaking the silence.

Grace thought of Howard and Wanda. Howard's devotion to his wife had truly touched Grace. "I saw something beautiful today."

"Oh?"

"Howard and Wanda Reeves checked in earlier," she explained. "I saw Howard taking care of his wife when it was obvious she couldn't care for herself." That was the best way she could think of to say it. "I could see it on his face that it wasn't an obligation. He simply adored her. It was truly lovely."

"That's the way it should be," Spencer said. He reached over and squeezed her hand.

Grace sighed, content.

They finished their meals in companionable silence.

"It was amazing," Grace said, pushing her empty plate aside.

"I'm so glad you liked it," Spencer said.

It was late by the time they left the restaurant. She didn't want the night to end, but she had to get up early in the morning to tend to her guests.

"I wish I could keep you out later," Spencer said as they strolled to his car, "but I know you have to work in the morning."

She smiled at him. "You must be a mind reader. I was thinking the same thing. I've enjoyed this evening so much."

"I have too." He unlocked the car and opened the door for her.

She got into the passenger seat. "I'm glad."

Spencer slid behind the wheel, then drove out of the parking lot and headed to Magnolia Harbor. During the drive, they discussed the books they were currently reading.

When they arrived at the inn, Spencer said, "I don't want to go another week before I see you. Would it be possible for us to have dinner again soon? I could cook for you at my house."

"I would love that. When?"

"Tomorrow is pretty busy for me. Maybe Wednesday?"

Grace thought about it. The medical conference would still be going on, but there would be no new guests. She could get Winnie or Charlotte to help out. "I think that would work great. What time should I get to your place?"

"Why don't we say five o'clock?" he suggested. "We can enjoy a nice relaxing evening. Maybe take a walk."

"Five sounds perfect."

"If you're a little late, that's fine." Spencer gazed into her eyes. "You're worth waiting for."

His meaning was unmistakable. He had waited for her, and he would continue to wait until she was ready.

"You won't have to wait." Grace leaned over and kissed him. It was on the tip of her tongue to admit that she loved him, but she refrained. The timing didn't feel right. "Thank you for a wonderful evening."

"I'll see you Wednesday," he said.

She got out and climbed the front steps. She knew Spencer wouldn't leave until she was safely inside. He took such good care of her. That was one more reason why she loved him.

Grace entered the mansion and waited until his headlights pulled away and disappeared. Then she walked to her quarters.

Winston greeted her at the door.

Grace scooped up the dog and cuddled him. As she relived the lovely evening, her heart overflowed with gratitude for Spencer and how happy he made her feel. "I can't wait to see Spencer again," she told Winston. "Do you think I'm acting like a schoolgirl?"

He yipped, wagging his tail.

11

Grace

Grace awoke Tuesday morning in a cheerful mood. And it was all because of Spencer.

Her heart soared as she recalled their date last night. She couldn't wait to see him again.

Grace stayed in bed, thinking about the day ahead. She had a few more Christmas gifts for Winnie and Charlotte that she wanted to pick up. She had already bought a present for Jake.

What should she get Spencer? She had searched in every shop in town for a Christmas gift for him. Everything was either too personal or not personal enough. She wanted a gift that showed how much he meant to her.

Was it too soon? They'd been dating for only a few months, although if she hadn't been so foolish this past summer they would've been dating longer.

Regardless of how long they'd been dating, she had never felt closer to anyone than she felt to Spencer. She'd certainly never felt this close to Hank. Not even when they were first married. She'd been young and in love, and she'd believed she knew what life was all about.

The feelings she'd had for Hank seemed shallow to what she felt for Spencer. Maybe it was their age. Maybe it was the experiences they'd been through. But somehow their relationship seemed to be richer and more vibrant.

Grace chided herself. She couldn't spend the whole morning

daydreaming about Spencer. She had a list of things to get done and guests to care for. She sighed and got out of bed.

Winston was curled up in his dog bed. He stretched, but he remained where he was.

After taking a quick shower, she opened the closet and contemplated her wardrobe. She was in a festive mood, and she needed something with a little sparkle.

Grace ended up dressing in a black pencil skirt and a red silk V-neck blouse. Around her waist she fastened a slim gold belt.

She kept her jewelry simple with a delicate gold chain necklace and gold hoop earrings with tiny bells attached to them. After sliding the earrings on, she tilted her head, and the earrings jingled. Grace smiled. Honestly, that was half the fun of wearing them.

Winston was still snoozing in his dog bed.

"I'm ready to go," Grace told him. "What about you?"

Winston jumped out of his bed and yipped.

She laughed at his enthusiasm. "We have no new guests arriving, but today's still going to be busy." Humming, she strolled to the kitchen, her faithful companion at her side.

Charlotte was removing a pan of blueberry muffins from the oven. She set it on top of the stove and turned to her sister.

"How are you on this beautiful morning?" Grace asked with a smile.

"You're certainly in a cheerful mood." Charlotte raised an eyebrow. "It wouldn't have anything to do with a certain handsome neighbor, would it?"

Grace grinned. "Maybe. But I'll never tell."

Charlotte laughed as she retrieved bacon and eggs from the fridge.

After greeting Charlotte, Winston made a beeline to his food bowl.

Grace poured kibble into the bowl, then freshened his water.

Wagging his tail, Winston dug into the food as though he hadn't been fed since last week.

Grace laughed softly. The sound of his teeth crunching into his dog food reminded her of a very small jackhammer. She glanced around the room. "What can I help you with?"

"How about toast?" Charlotte suggested. She was cooking scrambled eggs and bacon.

Grace walked to the fridge and removed the bread, then slid a couple of slices into the toaster.

"So how was your date last night?" Charlotte asked.

"It was wonderful," Grace answered. "He took me to that new hibachi restaurant."

"I've wanted to check that place out since I heard it was going to open," Charlotte said. "How was it?"

"Delicious," Grace said. "And the chef was incredible."

"I can't wait to go," Charlotte said. "I'll have to see when Dean is free."

"I think you'll both really enjoy the food and the whole experience," Grace said. "Spencer asked me over for dinner Wednesday evening. Do you mind? I hate to leave you alone for hospitality hour."

"It'll be fine," Charlotte said. "If I need any help, I'll call Winnie. Go ahead and enjoy yourself."

"Thanks," Grace said. "I appreciate it."

They worked in silence for a few minutes.

After Charlotte plated the bacon and eggs, she remarked, "You're being awfully quiet. Is there something you're not telling me about last night?"

"Let's go feed the hungry guests before they start banging on the kitchen door."

Charlotte rolled her eyes. "You really are high-spirited today."

"I have a lot to be happy about."

"Now I'm really curious. What's the big secret?" Charlotte walked around the island to confront her sister. "Did Spencer propose to you or something?"

Grace set the toast on a platter and added an assortment of jelly to a small basket. "Spencer hinted that he was thinking about the future. At least I thought that's what he meant."

Some of her exuberance suddenly died. In the light of day, it wasn't as clear as she'd thought it had been.

"Did he tell you he loves you?" Charlotte asked.

"No," Grace said. The longer she reflected on their conversation, the more doubts began creeping around the edges of her mind. "Not exactly. It was evident that he cares for me very much."

"That's good," Charlotte said.

"Actually, I think I said more about my feelings than he did about his."

Had Grace said she loved him? The sentiment had been there in her heart and her head the whole time they were together. She'd caught herself ready to tell him, but she didn't think she had. Had she told him with other words or in other ways?

What if he didn't mean that he loved her and was thinking about a future together?

"Stop." Charlotte walked over and rested her hands on Grace's shoulders. "I can see your mind spinning. It's obvious that Spencer loves you. He's considerate too. If he didn't have strong feelings for you, he wouldn't leave you wondering. He's too much of a gentleman for that."

As Grace considered her sister's words, some of her anxiety drained away. Charlotte was right. Spencer was a good man. If he wasn't serious, he wouldn't act the way he did when they were together. There would be no kisses or warm embraces.

Grace realized she was acting ridiculous, so she focused on assisting Charlotte with breakfast.

But doubts about Spencer's feelings for her continued to flood her soul.

Sam

After his alarm went off Tuesday morning, Sam stayed in bed for a few minutes reviewing the previous evening.

The keynote speaker was dynamic and a wealth of information, and he looked forward to hearing more from her in the coming days. But he didn't dwell on the conference. Instead, his mind was more pleasantly occupied with thoughts of Alyssa's smile and her laughter.

They'd sat next to each other during the keynote address. It had started with an innocent whispered comment Sam had made when the doctor behind them would not stop texting. Every ten seconds or so, his phone would chime with a new text. Even worse than that, every keystroke he made while responding created a sound.

After fifteen minutes of listening to the man's phone, Sam was done. "Hey," he whispered to Alyssa, "you think you can go back there and show him how to work his device settings?"

Alyssa had covered her mouth, but he'd still heard the snicker she couldn't hold in.

"Maybe we can find a teenager to sit with him and help," he added.

She giggled, then slapped her hand over her mouth.

Encouraged, Sam had continued making outrageous suggestions and comments.

After his third comment, she got into it and joined him. He decided that he would give anything to see her eyes sparkling like that on a daily basis.

Sam had felt bad about it. Mainly because he knew that they were being disruptive, just like the guy behind them. But he felt better when he realized the people around them were laughing too.

In order to cut down the noise, he'd pulled out his phone, which was on vibrate, and texted Alyssa. *This is how it's done.* He set his phone aside and pretended to be watching the speaker. In reality, he was waiting impatiently for her to read the text.

After that, they had exchanged messages all evening. Soon they stopped mentioning the poor guy behind them, and they were simply having a private conversation.

It was the most fun he'd ever had at a conference.

Sam glanced at the clock. He'd be late to meet Alyssa for breakfast if he didn't get moving. Throwing back the covers, he swung his feet over the edge and checked his phone. He smiled when he saw that she had sent him a text ten minutes ago.

I'm up. Determined to be on time today.

I'm going to hold you to it, he replied.

A moment later, she answered, *Game on.*

Grinning, he got up and went to get ready. As he shaved, he was careful not to cut himself in his excitement. That would ruin the impression he was trying to make. He needed to help her see past the best-friend image she apparently had of him.

Sam entered the dining room with five minutes to spare. He was the first one to arrive.

A few minutes later, Alyssa walked in. Her sly expression dissolved into a playful pout. "I thought I'd beat you here."

Sam laughed. "Sorry." He glanced at the clock. "Actually, I'm impressed. You're one minute early. I don't think that's ever happened before."

She snickered. "I shouldn't admit this, but I practically ran downstairs from my room. I didn't want to give you yet another reason to make fun of me."

"You'd do that to me?" He put his hand over his chest as if wounded. "Take away my fun?"

Alyssa laughed.

Grace and Charlotte breezed into the dining room with platters of bacon and eggs and a tray of croissants and muffins. They arranged the food on the sideboard next to a coffee carafe and a pitcher of orange juice.

"Sorry to keep you waiting," Grace said. She gestured to the sideboard. "Please help yourselves."

"Let's grab a plate," Alyssa said to Sam. "I'm starving."

"Not me," he said, but then his stomach growled.

Laughing, they walked over to the sideboard and made their selections.

After Sam and Alyssa sat down at the table, the other guests filed into the room and filled their plates. Charles and Savannah sat down with Marcie. Howard and Wanda took seats on the other end of the table, slightly away from the others.

Sam waved at Howard and Wanda.

Howard waved back, a weary smile on his face.

Normally, Sam would have gone over to exchange a few minutes of small talk, but he got the feeling they wanted to be alone, so he remained seated.

Sam couldn't remember ever enjoying a breakfast so much. His relationship with Alyssa had changed since he'd picked her up yesterday. Before then, they'd always had the memory of Derek with them. Most of their conversations had involved him in some way. They'd been friends for years, but Derek had seemed to keep them together.

Sam had worried that without his late best friend, he'd lose Alyssa.

But now he felt they were making strides in their relationship. At times, a look flashed over her, and Sam imagined she was finally seeing him for himself. His heart pounded in his chest like a drum.

He hoped the change remained after they got home. Maybe she could learn to have feelings for him too. He was willing to wait and let her catch up.

They finished their breakfast and walked to the barn for the conference.

"Think cell phone guy will have his phone silenced today?" Sam asked. He pulled a pack of gum out of his pocket and offered it to Alyssa.

"Spearmint's my favorite. Thanks." She popped a piece into her mouth and handed the pack back to him.

When her fingers scraped across his palm, his mouth went dry. Sam wondered if she could feel the connection between them. He glanced at her and noticed that her eyes were wide.

Yes, she felt something. Sam needed to play it cool because she seemed a little freaked out about it.

"I don't think he knew we were talking about him last night," he said, continuing the conversation as if nothing had happened.

"What? Oh yeah, I think you're right. He seemed pretty clueless yesterday."

Sam was encouraged that she'd sounded flustered because that meant she wasn't indifferent. He focused on making her laugh. He liked how easy it had been when they were having fun together. By the time they entered the barn, she was laughing at his antics.

"I can't believe it. I had no idea you'd be here."

His laughter died when he recognized that voice. Sam had never wanted to hear it again.

Justin Phillips stood before him, oozing confidence. "It's been a long time."

Not long enough. "I'm surprised to see you too," Sam said. They'd been rivals in medical school, and Sam had purposefully lost contact with him after graduation.

"Oh, I thought the training sounded interesting," Justin said. "I'm making quite a name for myself in the field, you know."

Sam held back his sneer. When he noticed Justin gazing at Alyssa, his heart fell. Justin had never met Alyssa because she'd attended a different medical school. Justin hadn't met Derek either. While Sam and Justin had entered the medical field, Derek had gone into business and become an actuary.

Alyssa blushed at the attention Justin was giving her.

She never blushed with Sam. A sick feeling clawed into his gut. Had he misread her interest in him? He wasn't blind. He knew that Justin was more attractive than he was. In med school, Sam had usually gotten better grades, but Justin had been blessed with a natural charisma and a silver tongue. He'd been everyone's favorite, and he'd known it.

"Aren't you going to introduce me?" Justin asked Sam.

He wanted to say no, but he couldn't be rude. "Alyssa Larson, meet my nemesis from med school, Justin Phillips."

Both Alyssa and Justin laughed, as if he had said something amusing.

Sam had been completely serious, even if it hadn't been an appropriate remark.

"Ladies and gentlemen, we're about to begin," someone said.

Sam scanned the room. "We should find seats."

Unfortunately, Justin insisted on joining them. Sam sat down, and Alyssa sat next to him. Justin sat on the other side of Alyssa.

Last evening Sam had taken great pleasure in keeping Alyssa entertained. Today he didn't get the chance. Every time he tried to engage her attention, Justin broke in and distracted her. Within an hour, Sam gave up.

The worst thing was, Alyssa seemed to like the attention from Justin. Sam hadn't felt so morose in a long time. As the morning wore on, his hopes that she was starting to feel something for him dwindled.

Sam and Alyssa had planned on sitting together for lunch. At least he had that to look forward to.

Finally, they broke for lunch, and Sam and Alyssa sat together at one of the tables. Of course, Justin followed them, and he took the seat across from Alyssa.

It was going all right until Sam left the table to get a can of soda. When he returned, Justin had slid into the seat beside Alyssa. All the other seats at the table were taken.

Justin smirked at him, and Sam fumed.

Alyssa turned to Justin. "Sam's back, so I'll talk to you later."

Justin's mouth dropped open, and so did Sam's. Women didn't usually tell Justin to move over for other men. But Alyssa did. The tightness around his heart loosened. Maybe Alyssa wasn't as fooled by Justin as he had thought.

Justin smiled tightly as he stood. "Of course. Enjoy your lunch, kids." He strode away.

Without Justin there to poison Sam's mood or monopolize Alyssa, they returned to their easy camaraderie. His worry about Justin coming between what might have been developing between them faded. He wasn't usually paranoid, but his emotional connection to Alyssa seemed to be messing with his common sense.

Sam briefly thought about Derek. He hadn't minded Derek pairing up with Alyssa. Okay, that was a lie. Yes, it had bothered him. Of course it had. Sam had been in love with her for years. But he had accepted it without a fight because it made sense. And he knew that Derek was an honorable man who would always put Alyssa first.

Seeing them in love had hurt, but in a weird way, it had also been a relief to know that the two people he loved most in the world were happy.

If Alyssa got together with Justin, Sam would never feel that way. Justin had been selfish as long as Sam had known him. Sam was certain that Justin would never put Alyssa's needs ahead of his own.

Sam knew that if he could ask Derek, his best friend would give him his blessing and beg him to protect Alyssa from Justin.

When lunch was finished, Sam and Alyssa walked around for a few minutes before returning for the afternoon session. To his relief, Justin didn't join them.

"I wonder if your friend is coming," Alyssa remarked. She sounded mildly curious. "Should we save him a seat?"

"No, I wouldn't worry about it," Sam said as he scanned the area. "I don't see him. He probably knows many of the other doctors here. I'll bet he found some colleagues to sit with." He wasn't disappointed in the slightest that Justin had disappeared.

They sat together, this time not talking.

He didn't mind. He could sit in her presence like this for hours. Simply being near her was enough.

At one point during the conference, Sam shifted his weight, and Alyssa moved at the same time. They ended up sitting with their shoulders touching. He stilled. So did she. He waited to see if she was going to move.

When she didn't, he peered at her. She was watching him.

Sam smiled at her, and she returned his smile.

His heart lifted as if someone had filled it with helium. It was all he could do to sit quietly, but he forced himself not to move.

This was a moment he'd remember all his life.

13

Charles

Charles drove Savannah to Winnie's house Tuesday afternoon. His daughter had been talking about spending time with Winnie and her cat all morning. But he worried briefly about how Savannah would communicate with Winnie.

His daughter would probably do better with Winnie than she did with her grandparents. Neither of them had ever considered learning sign language. Not a single word. It wasn't that they weren't capable. Louis and Margaret were as sharp as most people who were twenty years younger than them. They simply didn't want anyone they knew seeing them using sign language. They were embarrassed by the fact that Savannah didn't speak. Charles had a vivid memory of Joanna coming home after going out to a store with her mother. Joanna had signed to Savannah, and Margaret had demanded that she stop.

And that was the real reason they'd been harassing Charles. It had nothing to do with their concern for their granddaughter and everything to do with their own status and how people perceived them.

It was also why they hadn't wanted Joanna to marry Charles in the first place. He had gotten along with them, but he'd never been under the illusion that they approved of the marriage. Joanna was the daughter of a very wealthy man, and at the time, Charles had still been at the bottom of the ladder.

Winnie lived less than a mile from the inn, so it was a quick drive.

When he pulled into the driveway, Winnie came outside and waved at them.

Charles waved back, then opened the back door to get Savannah out of her booster seat.

She smiled at him.

His heart full, he leaned down and kissed her forehead. "Come on, munchkin," he signed. "Let's not keep Winnie waiting."

"I'm excited to see the cat," Savannah signed as she bounced out of the car.

"I know." Taking her hand, he led her over to Winnie. "Thanks for doing this. Savannah is anxious to play with your cat." He made sure to sign everything he said so Savannah could follow the conversation.

"Follow me." Winnie nodded at Savannah. "As long as you're gentle, Phoebe shouldn't mind." She led them in through the back door. They stepped into a utility room with a washer, a dryer, and a bench.

Charles glanced around and was pleased to note there were no chemicals anywhere. "I'm glad to see that Savannah can't reach anything harmful."

"Don't worry about dangers here," Winnie said. "My house has been thoroughly childproofed for my grandchildren."

He relaxed. "Sorry. I didn't mean to be offensive. I just needed to check. Especially since you might have trouble understanding Savannah."

Louis and Margaret hadn't childproofed their home. They felt children needed to learn where the dangers were. Foolishness. But they refused to listen to anyone.

A gray, black, and white tabby jumped off a chair as they entered the living room. The cat wound her way around Winnie's legs, meowing. He could hear the cat purring from where he stood.

"Here's my Phoebe." Winnie smiled and picked up the cat. "I adopted her when she was a kitten."

Savannah's eyes were wide. "She's so pretty." Reaching out a hand, she touched the brownish splotch across the cat's nose.

Phoebe sneezed.

Charles and Winnie chuckled.

"Does she have a sneeze spot?" Savannah signed.

"No, she doesn't," he signed. "That was an accident." *Coincidence* might be a hard word for her to understand. She was only five.

Winnie set the cat down on the floor.

Immediately, the feline started to twine around Savannah's legs, rubbing her head against the child. Savannah plopped down on the floor and gathered the cat into her arms. The cat pressed her head against Savannah's shoulder, begging to be cuddled.

"Looks like Phoebe has a new friend," Winnie said.

Charles nodded. "Thanks for watching Savannah. My meeting will last a couple of hours at the most. I'll come straight back."

"My pleasure," Winnie said. "If the weather's nice, Savannah and I will probably walk to the inn later. That way she can see Winston, and you can meet us there."

"I'll call you before I leave the restaurant to see where you are."

"That's a good plan. Don't worry about us. I've raised four daughters and have experience spoiling my grandkids. Savannah will be fine."

Charles didn't doubt it. If he did, he wouldn't have brought her here. Kissing his daughter's cheek, he told her to be on her best behavior. "I'll see you soon."

"Have fun," Savannah signed.

Not likely. She didn't realize that when he went to work, it was not fun like her preschool.

He drove to Aunt Patsy's Porch, a restaurant that promised Southern-style home cooking, to meet his client Ruth Gardner for a late lunch. About ten minutes later, he arrived at a white clapboard building with red shutters and a wide veranda wrapping all the way around it.

When he entered the restaurant, he scanned the dining room. The walls were lined with vintage photos and shelves filled with various antiques. The tables and chairs were mismatched, and there were lace curtains on the windows.

Charles spotted Ruth at a table near the window and rushed over to her. "Sorry to keep you waiting," he said as he took a seat across from her.

"No need to apologize," she said. "I was a few minutes early."

"Welcome to Aunt Patsy's." An older waitress approached and gave them menus. "I'm Molly. What can I get you to drink?"

They both ordered iced tea.

"Coming up," Molly said, then hurried away.

When Molly returned, Charles ordered chicken and dumplings, and Ruth asked for a Caesar salad and a bowl of potato soup.

They made pleasant small talk while they waited for their food.

Soon Molly delivered their meals. "Here you go. Let me know if I can get you anything else." She walked away.

"I was impressed with your proposal." He opened the portfolio he'd brought in with him. "It was intriguing, and I believe it will have consumer appeal. I do have a few questions for you."

As they ate, they discussed her proposal at length. Ruth had solid answers to all his questions. She was also willing to accept his advice.

By the time their plates were cleared away and the bill arrived, Charles was satisfied that Ruth would be a good candidate to work with.

He smiled. "If the rest of the team is as impressed as I am, I think we'll be ready to send you an offer within the next two weeks."

"That sounds wonderful," Ruth said. "I appreciate your time." She removed her wallet from her purse.

Charles waved for her to put her money away. "This is a business lunch. I'm taking care of it."

After paying the bill, he stood and shook her hand. "Thank you. I'll be in touch."

Charles whistled as he walked to his car. Things were looking up. He called Winnie to tell her he was on his way.

"We're at the inn," she said.

"I'll meet you there."

"Savannah was a pleasure to have today," Winnie remarked. "Don't worry about anything."

That was exactly what he wanted to hear.

Charles was almost to the inn when his father-in-law called. His muscles tensed as he answered the call, letting it play over the hands-free system. "What can I do for you?" he asked, his voice flat. He didn't have time for the man's games today.

"When will you be home?" Louis asked.

Charles frowned. He didn't like the way Louis asked. He had a bad feeling about the phone call. "I'll be home in a few days. Why?"

"Margaret and I have decided that our granddaughter needs a cochlear implant. We've been researching it, and we found a clinic nearby. We'll even pay for it."

Charles couldn't speak. *They* decided? As if such a thing were their choice. He couldn't believe the man would think he'd be okay with that.

"Did you hear me?" Louis demanded.

"I heard you. I've told you before that Joanna and I never wanted our daughter to have a cochlear implant. I haven't changed my mind."

"I knew you'd be selfish about it," Louis said. "Think of the opportunities you're denying her."

"I'm denying her nothing," Charles insisted. "If she decides she wants an implant later, I'll revisit the issue. Right now, there's no need. She's fine."

Louis snorted. "You think she's fine right now? She doesn't even talk."

"She's fully able to communicate through sign. She's healthy and happy. She doesn't need a surgery that will upend her entire life as she knows it. Again."

"I don't think you understand," Louis said. "You know I have power and influence. I'm not above using my status to get custody of Savannah. If you don't—"

Charles hung up on his father-in-law. He would not listen to his threats any longer.

But that didn't stop him from worrying about what Louis would do. For the past six months, the man had been hinting that he wanted Savannah to come and live with them. It wasn't going to happen, but Louis wasn't exaggerating when he boasted about his power and influence. Was it possible that Louis and Margaret could take his daughter away from him?

By the time he pulled into the inn, his mood had grown dark. His whole life was centered on keeping his daughter safe and happy. He'd never imagined that a threat would come from Joanna's family. What kind of grandparents did that?

He pasted on a smile long enough to greet Savannah and thank Winnie. When Savannah said she wasn't ready to go to the room yet, he agreed, wanting to walk off some of his temper. He contained it for Savannah's sake.

She signed to him about how she'd played with Phoebe and Winston. He paid attention as well as he could. When she started kicking the soccer ball she'd brought with her, he stood back and watched her. She was his joy. He shoved his hands into his pockets. It was impossible to contemplate life without her.

Charles would fight his in-laws if they tried anything. Despair rose inside him. What if some jury or judge thought his wealthy in-laws would be better for his little girl? His fear was that people wouldn't understand his decision. He'd met others who felt that he and his wife were wrong. It seemed that people were either for cochlear implants or against them. He wasn't against them. He just didn't want that for his daughter. At least not until she could make the decision for herself.

He was so deep in thought that he didn't hear anyone walking up to him until Marcie called his name. He turned to her while keeping an eye on his daughter. "What's up?"

"Not much," Marcie said. "I saw you and thought I'd ask how your business meeting went."

Charles had been so consumed with his father-in-law's threats that he'd all but forgotten the meeting. The satisfaction he'd felt had been destroyed. Not that he needed to tell her that.

"It went well," he answered. "The client I met with had a proposal that I think my team will be enthusiastic about. It would be a good business move."

She tilted her head and studied him, deep furrows forming on her brow.

"What is it?" Charles asked.

Marcie shook her head. "I get the feeling that you've got something else on your mind. You're trying too hard to convince me that all is well in your world. But I've been a lawyer too long not to know when someone is hiding something from me."

"Wait a minute. You're a lawyer?"

"For now."

"What do you mean?" he asked. "Are you thinking of quitting?"

She shrugged. "I'm trying to decide if I can still practice law without my hearing. I might have to try a different branch of law. I'm not sure what I'm going to do."

"I'm sorry," Charles said. "I guess I didn't think about how hard that must be for you." He could tell she didn't like his sympathy. "I'm not pitying you. Honest."

"That's neither here nor there," Marcie said. "Are you all right? I can't hear you, but I'm still a good listener."

His first instinct was to politely decline her offer. After all, it was a private matter, and he hardly knew Marcie. But Charles stopped and reconsidered. Even though they'd recently met, he already liked her and enjoyed talking to her. Besides, he had no one else to confide in, and he was too entrenched in the situation to view it objectively. Maybe Marcie would be a good sounding board.

Charles realized that he wanted to tell her about his situation. Yes, he wanted her thoughts, but he was also tired of feeling so alone.

He took a deep breath. "I would like your advice if you don't mind."

14

Marcie

Marcie hadn't expected Charles to actually tell her what was bothering him. He gave the impression that he was capable of handling his own problems. But when she'd seen him standing there, he'd seemed lost. Like a man who really needed a friend, someone who would listen without judging. She could understand that feeling. So, she'd braved his rejection and approached.

"I'd be glad to give you advice if I can," Marcie said.

"I can't believe I'm doing this," Charles muttered.

She couldn't tell if he was talking to himself or to her. She waited.

"I don't usually talk about my marriage," he finally said. "Or my in-laws."

Marcie wanted to tell him that he didn't have to, but she held her tongue. If he needed to talk, she didn't want to discourage him. And in her heart, she really wanted to help him if she could.

"I need to back up a little," Charles said, running his hands through his hair. "I met my wife, Joanna, at a benefit dinner. I was part of the committee putting it on. She was from a wealthy and very connected family. Her parents didn't approve of me. They believed I wasn't good enough for their daughter, so they did their best to break us up. In the end, we defied them and eloped."

Although Marcie had read about things like that, she didn't think parents still acted that way. She admired him for sticking with the woman he loved. Brian sprang to mind. He certainly wouldn't have done the same. She pushed her thoughts away.

"Joanna had trouble getting pregnant. She had several miscarriages. We had begun to doubt she'd ever be able to carry a baby for the full term, and we were discussing adoption. Then she found out she was pregnant again. When she lasted past the first trimester with Savannah, we knew she was a miracle."

Marcie waited, letting him gather his thoughts.

"When Savannah was born, I can't even tell you how emotional we were," he continued. "She was so tiny, but the nurses claimed she was the loudest baby they'd ever heard. They do newborn hearing screenings at the hospital. They screened Savannah twice, and she failed both times. They told us we needed to get her evaluated by an audiologist."

She could only imagine how traumatic that would be.

"It was overwhelming," Charles admitted. "The audiologist said that Savannah was profoundly deaf. We were given several options. One of them was a cochlear implant."

"I've heard of those," Marcie responded. "I've actually considered that for myself. My doctor said I was a good candidate because I've heard before." She paused. "I didn't realize they would do cochlear implants on infants."

He smiled at her, but his eyes were sad. "Medicine is an amazing thing. Joanna and I discussed it at length, and we were tempted. We would have been thrilled if she could have heard. I have read about some inspiring stories. But we didn't want to put our baby through surgery."

She could understand that. Surgery could be extremely risky.

"Don't get me wrong," Charles said. "I know of several parents who have gone with cochlear implants, and they've had great results. I think implants are amazing, and they do a lot of good. But sign language was something I grew up with. I have a cousin who's deaf. To me, that was an equally valid choice. Joanna and I agreed to hold off and let Savannah make the choice of whether she wanted to get a cochlear implant when she was older."

"I know sign language can be challenging to learn," Marcie commented. "I remember a teacher once telling me that ASL has a complete grammar system, idioms, and everything. Before that I assumed it was simply using signs for English words."

He nodded. "You're not alone. And there are systems that do use English words and signs together. It's hard to talk and use ASL at the same time."

"Watching you and Savannah has shown me that ASL is absolutely beautiful."

"My in-laws don't agree," Charles said.

"Surely they want your daughter to be happy, don't they?" she asked.

He frowned. "They left the issue alone while my wife was alive. After she died two years ago, they started to hint at how wonderful it would be if Savannah got a cochlear implant. This afternoon, my father-in-law called me and said that he and his wife had decided it was time she had the surgery. They found a nearby clinic, and they offered to pay for it."

Marcie blinked, appalled. "That is about the craziest thing I've ever heard. You're her father, so it's your decision, not theirs."

"I agree, and that's what I told him," Charles said. "He claimed I was being selfish, and I was denying her opportunities."

She snorted. "If anyone's being selfish, it's him."

"I also told him that if Savannah wanted to get a cochlear implant when she was older, I would consider it," he responded. "I'm okay with her deciding she wants them."

"That makes total sense."

"I'm going to ask you something," Charles said gravely. "It may come out as rude, but I don't mean it to."

"All right," Marcie said, feeling slightly wary. "Go ahead."

"You could hear at least a little for most of your life, and now you've lost your hearing. You mentioned that you might get a cochlear implant. Do you think my decision was selfish? In your opinion as a lawyer, do you believe I've harmed my daughter?"

She understood what he was asking. "You can't compare Savannah's situation to mine. I once heard someone say that no two audiograms are alike. I think they meant it's the people who are different." Audiograms were the graphs that showed the results of hearing tests.

He nodded.

"What works for one individual will not work for another," Marcie went on. "As a lawyer, I see a father who provides for his daughter's needs. He is loving, conscientious, and cares for her. He is able to communicate with her fluently, and he is teaching her to advocate for herself. He's waiting on a major medical choice for her until she is old enough to contribute to the decision-making process." She grinned at him. "That self-advocacy thing was talked about at every IEP meeting I ever had, so it's pretty important."

An IEP referred to an individual education plan. It was a yearly plan that all the team members working with a child in the special education system followed.

"Thanks," Charles said. "I was afraid I'd lost perspective, and I needed to know that I wasn't harming her."

She bit her lip, wondering what he was holding back. It was clear that this conversation wasn't over. "What else happened?"

"He reminded me that he has power and influence, and he was not above using it." Charles shrugged. "So I hung up on him."

Her mouth dropped open. "So he threatened to sue you for custody?"

He sighed. "Yes, that's exactly what he did. I've sensed that it was coming, but it's still kind of a shock. I don't know what to do."

Marcie contemplated the situation. "I guess the first thing to do is research the benefits of sign language with young children. And start thinking about hiring an advocate."

"Like you?"

"No. Although having a lawyer would be a good idea too," she said. "An advocate is someone who specifically goes to meetings and stands in for Savannah, making sure her rights and needs are being met. The deaf community is an extraordinarily strong group that has been fighting for their rights for a long time. I'm not saying you have to hire an advocate yet, but I'd consider it."

"Do advocates really help?" Charles asked.

"They definitely do," she assured him.

They continued discussing the situation until it was nearly time for hospitality hour.

As they walked to where Savannah was playing, Charles asked, "Will you join us?"

"I'd love to," Marcie said. "Do you think Savannah can teach me a few more signs?"

He smiled. "I'm sure that can be arranged."

15

Sam

"That woman is a genius." Alyssa took off her reading glasses and slipped them into her laptop bag. Then she wiped her eyes.

"She is," Sam agreed, examining her face. Was she crying? How had he not noticed?

The other attendees milled around, and some headed for the door.

"Come on." Sam stood and stretched. He needed to get her out of here and find out what was going on. They'd been sitting for several hours. That would work as an excuse. "The caterers will be another twenty minutes getting dinner set up. My legs are cramped. I need to move."

"Let's go for a walk," Alyssa suggested. "The grounds are lovely."

"Good idea." Without thinking, he held out his hand to her, then froze. Was the gesture too revealing?

She smiled at him.

It was a sad smile that reached inside him and twisted his heart in its grasp. Sam almost withdrew his hand, but there was no way to do it without the moment getting even more awkward. He tried to convince himself that helping a woman to her feet didn't mean that much. Perspiration broke out on the back of his neck.

Finally, Alyssa put her hand in his and stood, her stare locked on his.

Sam held her hand a second longer than necessary before letting it go. If it was up to him, he'd hold her hand all day long, but he didn't want to press his luck. He opened his mouth, but his throat seemed to be blocked. Clearing it discreetly, he tried again. "So, where should we go?"

She averted her gaze and scanned the barn. "It seems like we're not the only ones leaving. I think it would be nice to walk around the lake for a few minutes."

"The lake it is."

They left the barn, neither of them speaking. As they strolled to the lake, a new energy buzzed between them. It wasn't tension. Not exactly. It was more of an awareness.

Sam became uncomfortable with the silence. Was she feeling the chemistry between them, or was she simply feeling uncomfortable? What if he had somehow damaged their friendship?

"I almost didn't come to this conference," Alyssa said.

"Really? Why?" Sam couldn't hide the surprise in his voice. They'd been planning to attend this conference for months, and she'd never hinted that she might cancel. A thought occurred to him. Maybe she'd considered backing out because of him.

Sam chided himself for behaving like a teenager. He was a mature man in his thirties. He needed to stop acting like he was still the painfully shy boy who'd been abandoned by his father when he was eight. He had proven that he wasn't a loser like his dad had claimed. He cared for his aging mother, and he'd landed a great job after paying his own way through medical school.

She shrugged. "It probably sounds silly, but I got scared."

He stopped walking and stared at her. "You were scared of going to a conference?" *With me?*

Alyssa stopped walking too. "Well, I wasn't scared exactly. Maybe anxious. I've been a widow for two years. When Derek died, I was numb. Then I was devastated. But I had my work to keep me busy. And you were amazing. Honestly, I don't think I could have survived without you."

Sam didn't reply. Instead, he inched closer, silently telling her that he was there for her. He was always there.

She sighed. "A few weeks ago, I realized that although I still missed Derek, I needed to let him go. It wasn't an easy thing." She paused. "But then I found something."

"You don't have to tell me if you don't want to," he said gently.

"I want to," Alyssa insisted. "I've been wanting to tell you since I found out."

"Take your time," Sam said, bracing himself for the worst.

"I was going through Derek's desk. I'd been putting it off because it felt too daunting. He'd gone to an oncologist without telling me." She paused, and when she spoke again, her words shocked him to his core. "Derek had cancer."

Surely he'd misheard. "Cancer?"

"So I was right. He never told you either."

"Never. If he had, I would have made sure he told you too." He was stunned. They had practically been brothers. Sam didn't think there was anything they hadn't told each other. "I'm so sorry. I never dreamed you were going through this. And here we are listening to a cancer specialist. I would have never brought you here if I'd known."

"Oh, hush," she said. "I know that."

"So you had no idea about his diagnosis?" Sam asked.

"No, but I think he was planning to break the news to me the day he died," Alyssa answered. "He called in the morning and suggested we go out to dinner. I knew there was something on his mind. The accident happened before he could tell me. Tell us."

It made sense. Obviously, Derek wouldn't have told Sam before Alyssa. "I feel terrible, knowing my best friend was going through that and I couldn't help."

"If you had known, I'm sure you would have done anything for him," she assured him. "And he knew it too. You were his best friend, and he thought the world of you."

"He adored you."

"I know, and I adored him." Alyssa rubbed her left ring finger. "But he would have wanted me to live. So that's what I'm going to do."

Sam didn't even think about it. He moved closer and gave her a hug. Not a romantic one. This embrace was all about comfort. There was love there as well, but there always had been.

Alyssa didn't pull away. Instead, she melted into the hug, accepting the comfort he offered.

Completely content, he stopped thinking. Stopped worrying. He allowed himself to be present and feel. It was a perfect moment.

When they broke apart, they both wiped their eyes and laughed. Sam wasn't ashamed that he'd shed a few tears with her. It was a cleansing experience.

"I think we should go back and eat," she commented.

He nodded. "Suddenly I'm starving."

Retracing their steps to the barn, they got into the buffet line.

Everything was especially tempting tonight. Sam helped himself to the salad, chicken fettuccine Alfredo, roasted potatoes, and green beans. Later if he had room for dessert, he decided to come back for a slice of French silk pie.

"Where should we sit?" Alyssa asked.

He scanned the room and gestured toward the far wall. "There are a few empty seats at that table."

They made their way across the room and sat down across from Howard and Wanda.

Howard greeted them with a warm smile. Wanda seemed more withdrawn, but Sam wasn't offended.

Sam and Alyssa tucked into their meals, chatting with Howard about where they worked.

Then Justin appeared and sat on the other side of Alyssa. He scooted his chair closer to her. "Hey, guys. I've been looking for you." His gaze never left Alyssa's face, making it clear who he'd really been searching for.

"I haven't seen you around this afternoon," Sam said, the words bitter in his mouth. He didn't add that he hadn't wanted to see him.

Howard gave Sam a sympathetic glance.

Apparently, Sam hadn't been able to hide his lack of enthusiasm for Justin's company.

But Justin obviously wasn't offended because he completely ignored Sam's remark and started relaying an amusing anecdote.

Sam tightened his jaw. He'd tolerated Justin in med school, and it had been rough. Aside from being rude, he didn't see any way to avoid him here. Sam reminded himself that the conference was only for a few days. He could put up with almost anything for such a brief time. He shouldn't let his old rival bother him. Instead, he should focus on being grateful for this time with Alyssa.

However, as the meal continued, his aggravation grew. Justin dominated the entire conversation. Whenever someone else started to tell a story, Justin interrupted with a better one.

Alyssa laughed at Justin's stories and jokes, but Sam couldn't tell if she did it because she was being polite or if she was truly amused.

Sam wasn't proud of it, but a few times he found himself referring to events or memories that belonged to Alyssa and him alone. Things that the others at the table would not have any connection with.

But Sam's attempts to talk to Alyssa didn't work. Justin always jumped in.

When Sam recognized that it was a hopeless case, he stopped trying. He'd seen Justin do this before. His old arrival was a pro at discouraging any competition. Right now, it was clear that Justin was competing for Alyssa's attention.

If Alyssa was developing feelings for Sam, then nothing Justin said would matter. Sam thought Justin sounded arrogant and rude, but he well remembered that Justin had been immensely popular with the opposite sex.

And Sam had always been invisible.

After everyone finished their meals, Sam was more than ready to get away, but he couldn't leave Alyssa alone with Justin. In addition to not liking Justin, Sam didn't trust him. Justin would not care if he broke Alyssa's tender heart. To him it was all a game.

For Alyssa's sake, Sam stayed and held his temper. But he wouldn't compete with Justin. If Alyssa couldn't see that Sam was the man who would love and cherish her, he couldn't do anything about it. At least not now. He needed to wait until he had the chance to talk to Alyssa alone.

"You're a very rude man," Wanda blurted out as she glared at Justin. Her lips were pursed, as if she were holding in a barrage of angry words.

Sam and the others gaped at the woman who had not said two words the entire meal.

Howard went a little pale.

Justin lifted his chin and sneered at Wanda. "Are you talking to me?"

Howard slid closer to his wife, putting a protective arm around her.

"I certainly am." Wanda sniffed. "I've watched you this entire time. You won't let anyone else get a word in edgewise, and all you do is talk about yourself. Anytime someone tells a story, you've done something better. Honestly, if you're so great, I wonder why you've deigned to sit here with us. Shouldn't you go find loftier people to socialize with?"

Howard settled a calming hand on her shoulder.

She ignored her husband as she continued to glare at Justin.

"As if anyone cares about your opinion," Justin responded. "I watch how people back away from you. Other than your husband, I don't think anyone here even likes you."

"Don't talk to my wife like that," Howard said tightly. The seemingly easygoing man didn't sound so mild-mannered now.

All the anger had drained from Wanda's face, and she appeared lost. Broken. Sam's heart twisted.

Justin threw down his napkin. "This is ridiculous. I'm heading back to my hotel." He stood up, then faced Alyssa. "I'll see you tomorrow, and we can talk about where we're going for dinner tomorrow night." He marched out of the barn.

Sam had a hollow feeling in the pit of his stomach. Alyssa had agreed to eat dinner with Justin tomorrow evening away from the conference? She'd never mentioned it to him. When she had talked about moving on, Sam had hoped she was referring to him. Now he felt foolish. Apparently, she'd been talking about Justin.

Although at the moment, she seemed close to squirming with embarrassment, and her cheeks were red.

Would she still go to dinner with Justin tomorrow? Then again, did it matter? Even if Alyssa had lost interest in Justin after his little show this evening, Sam doubted that she'd ever consider him as more than her old friend.

He should give up before he got his heart broken. But it was probably too late for that.

Alyssa stood. The blush had faded, making her skin appear paler than usual. "I need to find the ladies' room. Wanda?"

Wanda nodded and stood. "That sounds like a good idea."

Howard stood too. "Are you all right?" he asked his wife.

Wanda patted his cheek, still sad. "You take such good care of me. The man was rude, but maybe he was right about me."

Howard leaned in and kissed her forehead. "Don't believe a word he said. You're still the woman I married twenty-nine years ago. I love you as much now as I did then. That's the only thing you should listen to."

She gave him a single nod, then followed Alyssa.

With a heavy sigh, Howard sat down again.

Sam understood what was going on. He was tempted to leave the subject alone, but he decided to give the man a chance to open up to him. "My mother is one of the finest women I have ever known. She is strong and optimistic. She is also in the beginning stages of Alzheimer's. It's difficult watching someone you love start to lose parts of herself."

Howard stared down at the table.

Sam waited, wondering if he would respond.

Finally, Howard glanced at Sam, his eyes shiny with tears. "It began so slowly with minor things. Wanda would forget what she wanted to say, or she'd miss an appointment. It's been getting worse for the past two years. It used to be she'd have a bad day every now and again, and the rest of the time she'd act the same as always. But lately, her good days are coming less often."

Sam had started this conversation, but he wasn't sure how to proceed. He decided to stick with the simple truth. "I'm sorry for what you're going through."

"Thank you. For what it's worth, I don't regret marrying Wanda. Loving a good woman like her has been a true gift. Even if I'd known this was a possibility all those years ago, I still would have asked her to marry me. There are some things in life that are worth the risk."

Sam noticed the two women making their way back to them, and his gaze lingered on Alyssa. "But taking a risk might cost you more than you can bear to lose."

Grace

As Grace carried a fresh pot of coffee into the dining room on Wednesday morning, she thought about her upcoming date with Spencer. He had offered to cook for her, and she couldn't wait to enjoy dinner at his house. It would be more intimate than eating at a restaurant, despite how elegant the establishment was. But she couldn't help feeling a bit anxious. She still had doubts about his feelings for her.

Before she saw him tonight, she had to get through another busy day at the inn.

Charles, Savannah, and Marcie had finished their meals, and now Savannah was teaching Marcie new signs.

Grace watched as Savannah found a picture on a tablet, showed it to Marcie, and gave her a sign. Grace couldn't understand what the child was saying, but her expression was serious. When Marcie didn't copy a sign well enough to meet Savannah's standards, she had no problem correcting her, even though Marcie was more than a quarter of a century older.

Savannah picked a new sign. This time it was a butterfly. When Marcie attempted to imitate the sign, Grace thought it was spot-on.

Savannah shook her head and signed to her father.

Charles choked back a laugh and said to Marcie, "Savannah wants to know if you need me to come over there and sit with you and help you sign. Hand over hand."

Marcie's lips twitched, but she didn't smile. "I think I can do it. Give me another chance."

Savannah searched for another picture on the tablet.

While she was occupied, Marcie faced Charles. "She's more demanding than any teacher I've ever had."

Grace couldn't help but laugh as she walked over to the table. "I love that she's so into teaching you," Grace said to Marcie, then smiled and waved at the little girl.

Savannah waved back, then returned to the tablet.

"She's demanding, but she's actually a good teacher," Marcie said. "Better than I'd expected a child to be."

"Maybe so, but she'd terrify me if I was her student," Charles joked.

Grace held up the coffeepot. "Would you care for a refill?"

"Yes, thank you," Charles said.

Grace filled his cup.

Charles took a sip. "This is good coffee."

"I'm glad you approve." Grace wished them a good morning and moved on to the other guests.

Howard and Wanda were sitting together at the other end of the table. They were talking quietly, so she didn't want to disturb them.

Grace noticed that the couple was holding hands, and her heart melted at the way Howard gazed at Wanda.

Grace frowned when she saw that Alyssa was sitting at the table alone. That was odd. She approached the younger woman. "Good morning. How are you enjoying your stay with us?"

Alyssa stiffened. "Oh, good morning. It's a lovely place, and the conference is very informative."

Grace noted that she hadn't answered her question. She was suddenly concerned about her guest. "Coffee?"

"Yes, please."

Grace refilled her cup. "Is Sam joining you this morning?" she asked, keeping her voice gentle. She didn't want to pry, but she wanted to help in some way if she could.

"No, he's not," Alyssa replied, sounding rather confused. "We'd planned on eating together yesterday afternoon, but then last night, he changed his mind. He said he had something else he needed to do, but he didn't mention what it was."

That sounded like a man avoiding a woman. Grace wondered why. When they'd arrived at the inn, Grace could tell that Sam was in love with Alyssa. She had assumed Alyssa felt the same way. So why was he avoiding her?

If that was the case, there was nothing she could do about helping them. Perhaps they'd had a fight. Or maybe Sam really did have something he needed to do. The life of a doctor had to be stressful. Even when doctors were away, they presumably still had patients to care for and details to handle.

"Maybe he had something he needed to do for a patient," Grace suggested, unsure how to respond.

"Maybe," Alyssa said.

"If I can assist you in any way, please let me know," Grace said. There was nothing else she could do. If Alyssa wanted to talk, she'd listen. But she couldn't force the issue.

Excusing herself, Grace set the coffeepot on the sideboard and left the dining room. She went into the kitchen.

Charlotte was loading the dishwasher, and Winston sat near her feet, watching.

Grace laughed. "I see you have a supervisor."

"Not even a crumb can get past him," Charlotte joked. She turned and leaned against the counter. "Do the guests need anything?"

"No, there's plenty of food left."

"Good." Charlotte smiled. "Are you excited about your date tonight?"

"I am, but I'm a bit anxious."

"There's no need for you to worry about Spencer's feelings for you," Charlotte insisted.

"Do you really think so?"

"Yes, I do. You've been through a lot of emotional turmoil this year," Charlotte said gently. "It's understandable that you're worried."

Grace nodded. "You're right. I'm stressing over nothing."

"Relax and have a wonderful evening."

"I hate leaving you alone for hospitality hour again," Grace admitted. "Are you sure you don't mind?"

"Of course not," Charlotte said. "It's no problem at all."

"Thank you," Grace said, giving her sister a hug. "I still need to find Spencer a Christmas gift. I think I'll search for something online."

"Good luck."

Grace ducked into her private quarters, and Winston followed. She grabbed her laptop and sat down on the couch with the dog beside her. As she browsed, nothing called out to her as the perfect gift. And even if she did find something, would it arrive before Christmas? It was only nine days away.

She scratched behind Winston's ears. "Do you have any ideas?"

The dog licked her hand.

Grace shut down the computer. She'd have to try again later. There had to be something she could give him.

Most likely, Grace would have to return to the shops in Magnolia Harbor or drive to Charleston when she had the time. She was quickly running out of days.

If she waited too much longer, it would be a New Year's present instead of a Christmas gift.

17

Marcie

Marcie was having a wonderful time strolling down Main Street with Charles and Savannah.

Charles had gone to another business meeting in the morning, and Winnie had babysat Savannah again. After Charles had picked up his daughter, they'd returned to the inn and invited Marcie to join them for a visit to Magnolia Harbor. She had gladly accepted.

As they passed The Book Cottage, Savannah stopped and pointed.

Charles faced Marcie. "Savannah loves books. Would you mind if we checked the place out?"

"Not at all," Marcie replied. "I love reading too."

An older woman with brown hair greeted them when they entered. "Welcome to The Book Cottage. I'm Blanche. Is there something I can help you find?"

"I believe we're heading to the kids' section," Charles said, motioning to Savannah.

Blanche smiled. "Enjoy."

"Do you want to come with us, or is there another section you'd rather browse?" Charles asked Marcie.

She scanned the store. "I'd like to research ASL books, so I'll meet up with you."

Charles nodded, then ushered Savannah to the children's section.

Marcie went in the opposite direction and perused the titles. By the time she decided on one of the ASL reference books, she noticed

Charles and Savannah at the register, so she joined them. Marcie paid for her book and followed the pair out the door.

Savannah proudly showed Marcie the two books Charles had bought for her, and Marcie displayed the book she'd purchased.

"That will come in handy," Charles remarked.

"I hope so," Marcie said.

They continued walking down the cobblestone street. Marcie admired the majestic old trees and the charming shops decorated for Christmas. It was a lovely small town.

Savannah stopped and signed to her father.

"I believe I know that sign," Marcie said. "Is she saying she's hungry?"

Charles nodded. "Good job. You're picking up sign language very quickly. It's one thing to learn a sign, but being able to read the signs is another skill altogether."

Marcie blushed. "Thanks. I like learning sign language. When I go home, I want to take a class so I can keep studying it. My new book will help too."

She would miss Charles and Savannah when she returned home, and she hoped they wouldn't vanish from her life. She enjoyed their company, and she respected Charles. It was too early to tell if they could ever be more than friends, but she wondered if it was a possibility.

Not that Marcie was in a hurry to get involved in a new relationship. She was still bitter over the way Brian had betrayed her. He'd known there was a chance she would lose her hearing, so his actions had shocked her.

Now that she'd had some time to reflect, she recognized that Brian had always been selfish and insensitive of other people's feelings. At the time, she had been flattered that he had picked her. Looking back, she wondered if he had chosen her because he thought she was weak.

Charles checked his watch. "It is almost lunchtime. Where would you like to eat?"

Marcie had to ask him to repeat what he'd said, but it didn't embarrass her like it usually did. With Charles, it felt natural.

She realized that she'd gotten better at reading his lips. It was probably because she'd spent so much time with him the past couple of days. Once again, she contemplated how much she would miss Charles and Savannah when she went home.

Marcie quickly stopped that train of thought. She refused to waste these precious hours by lamenting something that hadn't even happened yet. There was no point. Instead, she planned to enjoy every last moment she had with them. The future would work itself out somehow.

"The Dragonfly Coffee Shop is great," Marcie said, "but they don't serve entire meals, only snacks."

"What are our other choices?" Charles asked.

Marcie checked the map of Magnolia Harbor that she'd gotten from Grace. "Why Thai is right down the street."

"Savannah is a picky eater, so I don't think that's the best option," Charles said. "I went to Aunt Patsy's Porch with a client yesterday. It was very good, and it has a large menu. All of us should be able to find something to eat there."

As Marcie read about the restaurant on the map, she felt herself grinning. "Evidently Aunt Patsy's Porch has the best pie in a hundred miles. I might skip the meal and go straight for the dessert." She couldn't believe how freely she was joking with him. At home, she was far more reserved with the men she knew.

Charles laughed. "Aunt Patsy's Porch it is." He winked at her. "I like pie too."

They walked to the car, and Charles drove to the restaurant. There was a short wait when they arrived, but Marcie was having such a great time that she didn't care.

Soon an older woman ushered them to a table. She passed out menus and a coloring book and a packet of crayons to Savannah. "Welcome to Aunt Patsy's. I'm Molly." She took their drink orders, then walked away.

"So, do you have another meeting tomorrow?" Marcie asked as she perused the menu.

"I do, but I might cancel it because Winnie's not available." Charles shrugged. "It was more of a courtesy visit with a current customer, so the meeting isn't necessary."

"Why don't I watch Savannah for you?" Marcie asked. She didn't know a lot about kids, but she and Savannah got along. It would help Charles, so she wanted to offer.

Before he had a chance to answer, Molly approached the table with their drinks. She gave a glass of milk to Savannah, an iced tea to Marcie, and a cup of coffee to Charles. Then Molly took their food orders and hurried away.

Marcie checked her phone for messages. When her notifications popped up, she saw two missed texts from Brian. With a sinking feeling in the pit of her stomach, she wondered what her ex-fiancé wanted. He had already made it clear that she was a liability to him.

Charles gently touched her hand.

Marcie looked up to find him watching her. Even Savannah had set her crayon down and was studying Marcie.

After shoving her phone into her pocket, she cleared her throat. "Sorry. Did you say something?"

Charles glanced at his daughter. When she started coloring again, he focused on Marcie. "What's wrong?"

She supposed she could try to pretend that nothing was wrong, but it would be a lie. Charles was perceptive, and she knew he wouldn't be fooled. But she didn't want to admit how bad her judgment had been. It was mortifying.

"I told you my problems about my in-laws," he reminded her.

Marcie removed her phone from her pocket, unlocked it, and scanned the messages. "It's from Brian, my ex-fiancé. I realize that I dodged a bullet when we broke up." Sighing, she passed her phone to him. "The last two messages."

As Charles read the messages, his jaw dropped.

"Yeah, that's what I thought too," she said.

"So, let me get this straight." Charles handed her phone back. "This man you were going to marry is demanding that you send him the engagement ring he gave you so he can sell it and put a down payment on the house you were going to buy together."

Marcie couldn't help but smirk. It all seemed so absurd. "Yes, and I'm tempted not to return the ring. I mean, legally it's mine. He gave it to me without any stipulations about what I could do with it if we broke up."

"He has a lot of nerve," he said. "He's not even asking. It's more of a command. Is that why you broke up?"

Marcie flinched.

"I'm sorry," Charles said. "I didn't mean to pry into your private life."

"No, it's okay." She took a deep breath. "Brian and I met in law school, and we hit it off. We both love to debate, and we had long, intense discussions."

Marcie paused as she considered how to explain when the problems began. "About two months ago, I got sick, and my hearing changed. You know how your ears get stuffy and things sound weird when you have a bad cold?"

Charles nodded. She could tell that he was already starting to figure out what was coming.

"I kept waiting for my hearing to return to normal, but it never did," she continued. "I could still hear, but it was different. I started missing things at meetings. If I hadn't been in denial, maybe I would have adapted sooner and figured out how to handle the situation. Anyway, Brian started to avoid me. He would text me and say he was busy. I think I knew that something was up, but I stayed quiet about it."

Marcie took a deep breath, bracing herself to tell the worst part of her story. "A few weeks ago, I woke up one morning, and I couldn't hear anything. I finally went to my doctor, but it was too late. He'd been warning me for years that one day I would lose all my hearing. I have what's known as a progressive loss. In high school I knew it was coming, so I dutifully learned how to lipread. But until it actually happened, I never believed it. After all, I went to the audiologist every year, and my hearing had stayed the same for several years in a row."

"I'm sorry," he said.

"I certainly never thought that Brian would react the way he did. When I finally convinced him to meet with me, I explained that I was completely deaf, and I needed to see his face in order to talk with him. I think he was deliberately turning away so I couldn't see his mouth when he spoke. Maybe it was some kind of test. I don't know." Tears threatened, but she brushed them away. Brian was not worth crying over.

"He broke up with you," Charles said, finishing her story.

She nodded. "Then he told my boss that I was a liability to the firm. He made a list of the comments I hadn't heard at our staff meeting. He figured out I was having trouble hearing before I told him. Apparently, he believes I can't be a lawyer because of my hearing loss."

"That's terrible," he remarked. "Did they fire you?"

Marcie liked the fierceness in his eyes. She could tell that Charles would fight for the woman he was going to marry, not try to destroy her. "No, they didn't fire me. My boss is too aware of the Americans with

Disabilities Act. He didn't argue when I asked for a leave of absence. I imagine he's hoping I'll decide to quit while I'm away for two weeks."

"Will you?" Charles asked.

"I don't know," she admitted. "I thought I would enjoy my job a lot more than I do. It hasn't been easy, even before I lost my hearing. I don't always agree with the way things work out."

"You still have time to think things through," he reminded her.

Molly sailed over to their table to deliver their meals. "Hope you folks enjoy your lunch. Let me know if you need anything." She rushed off to another table.

As they ate their meals, the conversation shifted, and Savannah joined in.

Marcie was fine letting the subject drop. She had given Brian enough of her time and energy. She pushed all thoughts of him and her job out of her mind and focused on enjoying her time with Charles and Savannah.

It would come to an end all too soon.

18

Grace

The day crawled by as Grace worked around the inn. She chided herself for feeling anxious about her dinner with Spencer. But the closer it came to five, the more twisted the knots in her stomach grew. She didn't remember being this anxious when she was dating Hank eons ago. She was almost fifty, and here she was mooning over Spencer like she was sixteen. Although when she'd been dating Hank, she hadn't yet learned how easily things could go wrong and dreams could get shattered.

"Am I crazy, Winston?"

The dog padded over and sat at her feet, gazing up at her.

"You're right. I'm being silly. I've been out with Spencer lots of times. There's no need to be anxious."

At four o'clock, Grace and Winston retreated to her quarters so she could get ready.

Grace dressed in a pair of jeans and an elbow-length black blouse with red flowers. She wore socks and sneakers, just in case she and Spencer decided to go for a walk. Then she tucked a red cardigan inside her large shoulder bag.

After applying her makeup, she said to Winston, "This is as ready as I'm ever going to be."

He wagged his tail and yipped.

"We should get moving," she said. "Let's say goodbye to Charlotte first."

Winston's nails clicked on the floor as he followed her to the kitchen.

"We're leaving," Grace announced. "Are you sure you're okay with hospitality hour on your own?"

"It's all under control," Charlotte said, removing chocolate cupcakes from the oven. "Winnie's stopping by."

"Thanks," Grace said. "Call me if you need anything."

"Enjoy your evening." Her sister waved her off.

Grace and Winston went out to her car in the parking lot. She opened the passenger door, and Winston hopped onto the front seat.

A short while later, she pulled into Spencer's driveway and parked in front of his white two-story farmhouse. She let Winston out of the car.

When they walked to the house, they were greeted by Spencer's chocolate Lab, Bailey.

Grace scratched the dog behind the ears, and Bailey wagged her tail in doggy delight.

The two dogs sniffed each other, then began frolicking around the yard.

Spencer opened the front door. "You're right on time. It's great to see you."

"You too."

He gave her a hug, and she melted into his embrace.

"I hope you're hungry," Spencer said. He ushered her through the house and to the rear patio, where the tantalizing scent of barbecued ribs sizzled in the air.

"The food smells wonderful," she commented. "Your ribs are the best."

At the mention of food, Winston and Bailey trotted over to them. When they realized Spencer wasn't offering any handouts, the dogs curled up next to each other for a nap. They had obviously worn themselves out.

Smiling, Spencer took her hand and escorted her over to the table.

Grace suddenly noticed that the table was set for a romantic dinner for two with fine white china plates, elegant glasses, and gleaming silverware. A crystal vase stood in the center of the table surrounded by twinkling candles, and a large bouquet of roses had been placed at her seat.

He gathered the flowers and presented them to her.

"Thank you. They're beautiful." Grace accepted the bouquet, feeling overwhelmed. What had she done to deserve such a kind, generous man?

"I'm glad you think so," Spencer said.

She glanced around. "Where should I put them?"

"I already thought of that." He pointed to the vase in the center of the table.

"Of course you did," Grace teased. She arranged the flowers in the vase, leaning close to smell their sweetness. "They're lovely."

Spencer led her to her seat and held the chair for her. He left her to fetch a large bowl of salad, baked potatoes, and the ribs from the grill. After setting the food on the table, he turned up the music.

She noted the lush, romantic strains and smiled at him.

Spencer had gone out of his way to create a romantic atmosphere. She felt special, sitting across from him as he poured her a glass of red wine.

As they relished their meals, they had a lively discussion about a movie they'd both recently watched. Then they caught up on what they'd been doing since their last date.

"Everything was spectacular," Grace said, pushing her empty plate aside.

"I hope you saved room for dessert," he said, a twinkle in his eyes. "I picked up an apple pie and vanilla ice cream."

She grinned. "I always have room for pie and ice cream."

They collected the plates and carried them into the kitchen. Spencer sliced the pie, and Grace scooped the ice cream.

Not for the first time, she considered what a good team they made. It felt natural working side by side in his kitchen. As she gazed at him, all her fears and worries faded from her mind, and she wondered why she'd been so anxious about this evening.

On the way out of the kitchen, Spencer grabbed two dog biscuits. "Bailey and Winston deserve their own dessert."

Grace smiled. "They certainly do."

They carried their plates of pie à la mode to the rear patio, and Spencer rewarded the dogs with their treats.

Grace and Spencer sat at the table, savoring their desserts in companionable silence.

"What a remarkable evening," she said, smiling at him. "Thank you."

"It's not over yet." He stood and held out his hand. "Will you dance with me?"

Grace placed her hand in his and allowed him to lead her away from the table. It felt wonderful swaying to the music with his strong arms around her.

The song ended too soon. Spencer stopped and took her hands in his.

Grace shivered at his touch. Suddenly, she felt anxious again, but she had no idea why.

Spencer leaned forward and kissed her. When he backed away, he kept hold of her hands. "I never imagined that I would meet anyone like you when I moved to Magnolia Harbor. You're kind, intelligent, and beautiful, and you can always make me laugh. You mean the world to me, and I treasure every moment we're together." He squeezed her hands. "I love you."

She blinked back her tears. "I love you too."

He released her hands, then removed a small box from his pocket and got down on one knee. As he opened the box, the light caught on a gorgeous diamond ring. "Grace Porter, will you marry me?"

She gasped. Was this really happening? "Yes, of course I'll marry you."

Smiling, Spencer pulled her into a tight embrace. "You've made me so happy," he whispered.

"And you've made me even happier," Grace said.

When they finally parted, he slid the ring onto her finger.

Joy bubbled up inside her, and she felt as if she'd float away. She could no longer fight the tears.

Winston and Bailey barked and ran in circles around their legs, offering their own form of congratulations.

Grace and Spencer laughed.

"I'm glad they approve," she said, wiping away tears of joy.

"Me too." Spencer smiled and leaned toward her, sealing their love with a sweet kiss that melted away all her anxiety.

They fit together so perfectly. She couldn't wait for their life to begin.

Charles

Charles sat with Savannah and Marcie on the rear veranda during hospitality hour. He had enjoyed their earlier outing to Magnolia Harbor and their lunch at Aunt Patsy's Porch, and he was glad that Marcie had agreed to join them this evening. They lingered over the food and drinks. Savannah thumbed through one of her new books while Charles and Marcie talked.

"It's so serene," Marcie said, gesturing to the lake. "If I ever buy a house, I want it to be close enough that I can watch the water when I need to think."

"We have a lake near our house." Charles leaned back in his chair. "It's a small man-made one. In the summer, Savannah and I go fishing, and sometimes we take out my little pontoon boat."

Marcie frowned. "I'm sorry, but I didn't understand everything you said."

He moved his chair so that his face was in better lighting, then repeated what he had said.

"Does Savannah know how to swim?" Marcie asked.

"Absolutely," Charles said. "We live near a lake, so she needs to know how to swim. She's been taking swimming lessons since she was four. I'm glad she loves the water. I think she gets it from me."

"How is everything this evening?" Charlotte asked as she breezed over to them.

"Wonderful," Marcie said. "I especially liked the stuffed mushrooms."

"I'm glad," Charlotte said. "Is there anything else I can get you?"

After Charles and Marcie declined, Charlotte excused herself to talk to the others. Sam was sitting at a table with Winnie, but Alyssa wasn't with them. Charles hadn't seen Howard and Wanda all evening.

Charles and Marcie sat quietly together, lost in their own thoughts as they watched the lake.

He recalled their conversation about Marcie's ex-fiancé during lunch. It took a lot to make Charles angry, and he liked to think of himself as even-tempered. But listening to Marcie talk about Brian had made his blood boil. What kind of man treated a woman that way? Even if Brian no longer wanted to marry Marcie, there was no reason to attempt to ruin her career or devastate her any more than he already had. The fact that Brian had gone out of his way to create a list of her so-called failures was nothing less than cruel.

After a few minutes, he broke the silence by touching her hand to get her attention. "I hope you know that you're better off without Brian. You're too good for him."

Marcie smiled faintly. "Thanks for saying that."

"Are you going to give the ring back?" Charles asked.

"I probably will," she said. "I don't know what I'd do with it anyway."

He tilted his head and observed her. "You could sell it."

"I've considered it," Marcie admitted. "But if I sold it, I'd always be bothered by it. I know it's rude for him to ask for it back, but he did pay for it. I'm not out anything by returning it. Except a fiancé, of course."

Charles scoffed. "Like I said, you're better off without him. He would have made you miserable."

"You're probably right."

"No probably about it," he insisted. "A man who would try to destroy a woman's career like that is not worth your time or your tears."

She wiped the tears from her cheeks. "I can't believe I was crying over him. Although I understand why he did it."

Charles blinked, confused. "How can you say that? What's there to understand?"

"Brian is extremely focused on his career," Marcie said. "When he realized I couldn't hear, he was afraid I'd embarrass him. I think part of him worried that I would hold him back. And I'm pretty sure that once he broke up with me, he was worried that I would be a reminder of his cowardice. He felt guilty."

He stared at her, not sure how to respond.

She shrugged. "Or maybe he was simply a jerk. That's possible too."

They both laughed.

Charles met Marcie's eyes, and a spark jumped between them. They gazed at each other for a moment.

Then Marcie got to her feet. Regret danced across her face and disappeared so fast that he could have imagined it.

But he knew he hadn't. He understood. It was too soon. Both of them had their own personal issues, and they'd met only a couple of days ago.

If their friendship lasted beyond this brief vacation, then someday they might explore a deeper relationship.

But not yet.

"I should return to my room," Marcie said.

"We'll walk upstairs with you," Charles offered. "Savannah needs to go to bed."

As if on cue, Savannah yawned.

They laughed.

Charles held his daughter's hand as he escorted Marcie to her suite on the second floor.

Marcie unlocked the door and smiled. "I had a nice time today."

"I did too." He touched her shoulder. "I'm sorry I asked so many questions. I hope you didn't think I was rude."

"I don't mind." Marcie blushed. "Actually, talking about it helped, and I feel better now."

"I'm glad," Charles said. Then he remembered something. "Were you serious about watching Savannah tomorrow while I go to my meeting?"

She nodded. "I'd love to. What time?"

"My meeting is at twelve. I'll leave here around eleven thirty. Should I bring her to your room?"

"That would work," Marcie said. She signed goodbye to Savannah.

The little girl smiled and signed in return. Then she signed something longer to her father.

Charles grinned. "She says you're getting better, and you should have more confidence in yourself. That will help to smooth your movements."

"Maybe she can give me some more tips on that tomorrow. I'll see you then." Marcie waved and went inside her room.

Charles and Savannah walked down the hall to their room. Soon his daughter was tucked into bed, where she fell asleep almost immediately.

But he was too restless to sleep. He felt uneasy that he hadn't heard anything from Louis today. His father-in-law was sneaky, and Charles knew him too well to imagine that he had given up. No, the man was simply biding his time.

He decided to take Marcie's advice and research an advocate for Savannah. Grabbing his tablet, Charles sat on his bed and searched the responsibilities of advocates. At first it made his head spin. There was too much information. He had to weed through various sites to find the material he needed.

When his neck began to ache, Charles checked the clock. He'd been researching for more than two hours. He still had more questions, but he'd taken some notes that would be a good place to begin.

Tomorrow he would run his notes by Marcie. Maybe she could add something and clarify a few details.

Setting his notes and his tablet aside, he climbed into bed, listening to his daughter's breathing from across the room. He settled in.

Charles had no idea what time it was when he jerked awake.

The dream had felt so real. Louis had snatched Savannah right out of his arms, and Charles had stood there, frozen. Appearing out of nowhere, Joanna had demanded to know why Charles had allowed her father to steal their daughter.

His legs were shaky when he got out of bed. He stumbled over to where Savannah still slept. She was there. She was safe.

No one was going to take his little girl away from him. If Charles had to sell his company to hire attorneys, then he would. His business didn't matter. The most important thing in his life was Savannah.

Marcie would help. Charles didn't know why he was so certain that she'd be instrumental in assisting him, but he was. He believed that things happened for a reason. It was too much of a coincidence that he and his daughter would run into a deaf lawyer here.

Knowing he needed more rest, Charles returned to bed, but his mind continued racing. He tossed and turned. Finally, he fell into a restless sleep.

When he woke again, the sun was streaming in the windows. Savannah was awake, signing to herself on her cot. He swung his feet out of bed.

Savannah saw him and flew over for a hug.

Charles held her tight, feeling so blessed to have her. "Let's get ready for our day. You're going to spend some time with Marcie while I go to a meeting," he signed to her.

"Good," she signed back. "I like her. She's nice. But she signs funny."

He chuckled. "She's still learning. Be patient."

"Will she come to see us when we go home?"

"I don't know yet. Maybe."

"I hope so," she signed to him.

So do I.

20

Grace

Grace woke up Thursday morning with a smile on her face. Just remembering her evening with Spencer sent joy flooding through her. She still couldn't believe they were getting married.

Feeling happier than she had in years, Grace got ready for the morning.

Winston seemed to be in tune with her cheerful mood. He was more playful than usual, making her laugh as he played tug-of-war with his bed. The bed won.

She checked her phone and noticed a message from Spencer. *Good morning. I can't wait to see you. How about a coffee date later this morning? Love you.*

Smiling, she typed a response and invited him over after they served breakfast to the guests.

"Ready?" Grace asked Winston. She slid on her engagement ring. She couldn't wait to show her sister.

Winston bounded into the kitchen ahead of Grace as if announcing her presence.

Charlotte took one look at her and grinned. "You're glowing," she teased, a twinkle in her eyes. "Sit down, and tell me what happened last night."

"I need coffee first," Grace said, "and then we'll talk."

"There's a fresh pot," Charlotte said.

Grace poured a mug of coffee, then joined Charlotte at the island, keeping her left hand out of sight.

Winnie breezed into the kitchen and hugged both her nieces.

"I'm so glad you're here," Grace told Winnie. She was pleased that she could share the big news with her sister and her aunt at the same time.

Winston yipped and bounded over to Winnie.

"I'm excited to see you too." Winnie laughed and patted the dog's head. "I decided to go on an early walk, and I thought I'd stop by and see if I can help with breakfast. Are we taking a break?"

"Sort of," Charlotte replied. "Grace was getting ready to tell me about her date with Spencer last night."

"Oh, I want to hear too." Winnie perched on one of the stools.

"Spencer invited me over to his house for dinner," Grace began. "He barbecued ribs and set up a table on the back patio with candles, a bouquet of flowers, and lovely music."

"Sounds romantic," Charlotte gushed.

"It really was," Grace said. "After dinner, he asked me to dance."

"How sweet," Winnie remarked.

"When the song ended, he said he loved me." Grace raised her left hand, showing off the engagement ring. "And then he proposed."

Charlotte squealed and pulled Grace into a tight embrace. "I'm so thrilled for you. I knew Spencer loved you. You were worried over nothing."

"It was hard not knowing," Grace said. "It made me doubt myself."

It was Winnie's turn to hug Grace. "Congratulations, dear. I'm so happy that you and Spencer found each other. You make a wonderful couple."

"Did you tell Jake yet?" Charlotte asked.

"No, Spencer and I decided to tell the kids together," Grace answered. "But we called them last night, and they're all free Friday evening. We're meeting at Spencer's for dinner. I can't wait to tell them."

"I almost forgot that Jake's coming," Winnie said. "I'm excited to see him."

"Me too," Grace said. Jake worked as a software programmer in Raleigh, North Carolina, so he wasn't able to visit them very often. "He's driving here Friday, and he'll go straight to Spencer's. I'm so glad he has a lot of vacation time. He'll be here until after Christmas."

"Where is he staying?" Winnie asked. "All the suites are full."

"Friday night he's sleeping at a friend's house," Grace said. "Then he can stay in the Wisteria Loft Suite after Sam checks out."

"I wish Mom and Dad were here," Charlotte said wistfully.

Grace grabbed her sister's hand. "I do too."

"They would be overjoyed," Winnie said, wiping away the tears from her eyes.

The women reminisced about Hazel, Winnie's older sister and Grace and Charlotte's mother, for a few moments. She had passed away years ago, but she was never far from their thoughts.

"When's the big day?" Charlotte asked. "What kind of dress will you wear? Where are you going on your honeymoon?"

Grace laughed. "He proposed last night. We haven't had time to make any decisions. Besides, we want to check with the kids first. It's important that we schedule the wedding when they can all get away from work and their other commitments."

"I'll do the food and help you plan the wedding," Charlotte offered. "I have so many ideas already."

"First, we need to feed our guests," Grace said.

Charlotte sighed and got up.

Grace and Winnie helped Charlotte finish preparing breakfast. As the women worked, they chatted about the proposal and the upcoming wedding.

Grace felt like she was floating on air. She was so thankful for her sister and aunt. They were clearly excited for her, and she knew they wished her and Spencer the very best.

Charlotte and Winnie carried the food to the dining room, and Grace remained in the kitchen to feed Winston.

When Grace entered the dining room, she was a bit concerned to see Alyssa eating breakfast alone.

A few minutes later, Sam arrived, but even from where Grace stood across the room, she could see the tension between him and Alyssa. Something had happened. After Sam made his food selections, he sat down across from Alyssa, and they had a quiet conversation.

Grace wondered what was going on. She noticed Winnie gazing at Sam. Her aunt had a knowing look in her eyes.

Grace turned her attention to the other group at the table. Charles, Marcie, and Savannah were once again sharing a meal. The two adults were holding an intense conversation. Charles referred to a notebook while showing Marcie some things on his tablet.

Every so often, one of them would glance at Savannah in a way that told Grace the child was a prominent part of their discussion.

The romantic in Grace wondered if there was a spark between Charles and Marcie. It seemed unlikely since they'd only recently met, but it would be interesting to see if anything developed several months or a year into the future. Grace smiled. Perhaps one day they would return to the inn together.

Howard and Wanda were the last ones to arrive. Wanda seemed a bit distracted.

"Please help yourselves," Grace said, gesturing to the buffet table.

After the couple filled their plates and sat down, Grace went over to check in with them. Howard held up their end of the conversation. When Wanda did participate, she sometimes repeated a question that they had already discussed. Grace smiled, not letting on that she'd noticed. Howard seemed grateful.

Leaving the couple to their meal, Grace joined Charlotte and Winnie in the kitchen.

"I need to run, girls," Winnie said.

"Thanks for all your help," Charlotte told her.

"Anytime," Winnie said, giving them both hugs. She smiled at Grace. "I'm so happy for you and Spencer. Congratulations."

"Thank you," Grace said.

Winnie left, and Grace and Charlotte returned to the dining room. All the guests were gone, so they tidied up.

"What are you doing this morning?" Charlotte asked.

"Spencer's stopping by for coffee," Grace answered.

"How nice," Charlotte said. "I'll be in the kitchen if you need me."

As Grace waited for Spencer to arrive, she did some paperwork at the reception desk.

Winston strolled over and settled down at her feet.

The front door opened, and the bell jingled. Spencer strode into the foyer carrying a bouquet of roses.

Winston bounded over to him, wagging his tail.

Spencer bent down and scratched behind the dog's ears. He smiled at Grace. "How's your morning?"

"It's much better now." She rounded the reception desk and approached him.

He laughed and handed her the bouquet.

"You just gave me roses last night," Grace said. "I can't believe you're giving me another bouquet."

"You deserve flowers every day," Spencer said.

"They're beautiful," she said, inhaling the lovely scent. "Thank you."

"My pleasure."

"Let's get our coffee," Grace suggested.

Winston led the way to the kitchen.

Charlotte was sitting at the island studying a cookbook. When she noticed them, she jumped out of her seat and rushed over to hug them. "There's the happy couple. Congratulations."

"Thank you." Spencer grinned. "I want you to know that as your future brother-in-law, I'll always be available to sample your new recipes, especially the desserts."

Grace smiled. "There are definitely perks to having such a talented chef in the family." She took a vase from the cabinet, filled it with water, and arranged the flowers.

"The roses are gorgeous," Charlotte said. She grabbed her phone. "Let me take a picture of you two with them."

Spencer put his arm around Grace's shoulders, and she held the bouquet in front of her.

Charlotte took a few shots and set her phone aside. "I made a fresh pot of coffee, and we have cinnamon raisin bread left from breakfast." She plated two pieces of bread.

"Thanks," Grace said, filling two mugs.

"I'm heading home to do some research." Charlotte picked up her cookbook. "Call if you need me." She lived in a charming cottage on the property.

When Charlotte was gone, Grace and Spencer sat down at the island with their snacks.

A thrill went through her as she realized that soon she'd be his wife, and she'd be able to enjoy coffee with him every morning.

"I'm looking forward to breaking the news to the kids," Spencer commented.

"I am too," Grace said. "I can't wait to share our happiness with them."

They chatted for a little while longer, and then Spencer stood. "I should get going. I know you have to work."

"I'll walk you out," Grace offered. She followed him out the back door with Winston on her heels.

He hugged and kissed her goodbye. "I love you."

"I love you too," she breathed.

He got into his truck and waved as he drove away.

Grace and Winston watched until the truck disappeared.

"Hope you had a nice coffee break," Charlotte said as she approached from the cottage.

Grace nodded.

"Oh, you have to see the photos." Charlotte found the pictures on her phone and showed them to her sister.

As Grace studied the pictures, she smiled. She knew exactly what to give Spencer for Christmas.

21

Sam

Sam finished stuffing his clothes into his bag and attempted to close it. It was a tight fit. Grunting, he held the bag together with one hand and zipped it with the other.

He glanced around the suite one more time, making sure he hadn't forgotten anything. No, he had packed all his things.

Out of habit, Sam pulled his phone out of his pocket and unlocked it to check the notifications. His battery was almost dead. He normally charged it at night, but last night he'd fallen asleep without plugging it in. He should charge it for a while, but his car charger wasn't working right. He opened the side pocket of his bag to grab his charger, but the pocket was empty. Obviously, he'd left it somewhere. When was the last time he'd had his charger?

Mentally, he walked back through all the places he'd been yesterday. He'd brought his phone charger with him when he went to hospitality hour. He had probably left it on a table. He'd have to ask Grace and Charlotte if they had seen a charger. Hopefully, no one had walked off with it.

Frustrated, Sam yanked his bag off the bed and carried it to the door. He wanted to locate his charger and then go on his way. Every minute he was here, he sank deeper into the despair that had begun drowning him yesterday.

Part of him felt guilty for leaving Alyssa, but he doubted that she would even notice. Justin had been with her every time Sam turned around yesterday afternoon. He knew that Justin and Alyssa had gone out to dinner last night. Alyssa had asked him if it was okay. What could he say? He couldn't very well tell her that he loved her so she couldn't go out with Justin. Besides, he had no idea how she'd respond to the truth he'd hidden from her for so long, even if his confession wasn't tied to something as ugly as jealousy.

Unbidden, the image of Howard and Wanda came to mind. Howard's words had been with him since they ate together, but Sam didn't see that he had much of a choice. Howard knew that Wanda loved him, even though the Alzheimer's was stealing her from him bit by bit. All Sam had ever had was Alyssa's friendship. He didn't think he could bear to lose that and have nothing.

This morning, Sam had joined Alyssa at breakfast, determined to be a good friend. He asked her how her date had gone. In his heart, he hoped she would say that she didn't think she was going to see Justin again.

"It was good," she'd said, obviously unaware that his hope deflated like a balloon. "Actually, I wanted to talk to you about something."

He really didn't like the sound of that. "Sure. You know you can talk to me about anything."

Alyssa had averted her eyes. "Well, the thing is, Justin asked if I wanted to stick around for another day and visit some of the museums and parks in Charleston with him. I told him that I had come with you, but he said that you two were old friends and you wouldn't mind if he drove me home."

At that moment, his last kernel of hope had died. Sam realized that Alyssa would never see him as anything more than a friend. The ache in his heart was more than he could stand.

He'd smiled, hoping she couldn't tell that he was gritting his teeth. "That sounds like fun. If you're going home with him, I might take off early. I have things to do at home. In fact, I should go and start packing now. If I leave before lunch, I can miss rush hour."

She'd appeared shell-shocked.

He'd stood and turned to go, but he couldn't resist bending down and kissing her on the cheek. "Be happy."

Why had he said that? In retrospect, it sounded like dialogue from a cheesy movie. In his heart, he knew why he had said it. Despite how much her friendship meant to him, he could not stand aside and watch as she fell for another man. Especially a man like Justin.

Whether Alyssa knew it or not, their friendship was over, leaving a huge hole in his life. Sam was afraid that nothing would ever be able to fill it.

Sam felt terrible about lying to her. As a rule, he preferred the truth, regardless of whether it was comfortable or not. But he couldn't tell her the truth without possibly hurting her feelings or making her feel bad. As angry and miserable as he was, he still didn't want to put that burden on her.

He checked his watch, wondering if Alyssa and Justin were sitting together now. He remembered the first evening at the conference, the way he and Alyssa had goofed off during the entire keynote address. Did she laugh like that with Justin?

Impatient with himself, Sam shook his head. "Enough. There's nothing else I can do about it. I need to find my charger and go."

Picking up his bag, Sam left his room and headed to the stairway. He walked down the three flights of stairs. At the bottom of the stairs, he ran into Winnie. He had talked to her a couple of times during the last few days. He found her sweet, funny, and rather opinionated. He didn't mind that. Her liveliness made their conversations interesting.

Winnie glanced at his bag, then raised her eyebrows. "Are you leaving us?"

Sam squirmed under her gaze. He opened his mouth to tell her the same tale about how he had things to do, but he couldn't repeat that line again. For some reason, it was impossible to lie to Winnie. "Yeah, I'm heading home."

She nodded.

Why did he get the feeling she knew exactly what was going on with him? It was absurd, but he couldn't shake it.

"I understand." Winnie touched his arm. "Before you go, I have something for you."

Until that moment, Sam hadn't noticed that she was carrying his charger and a book.

She handed him both items.

"Thanks," he said, "but this isn't my book."

"I know it's not," Winnie said. "It's been weighing heavily on my mind this morning. I have the feeling that you need it." She smiled, then walked away without saying another word.

Sam stared after her. No one was in the foyer so he couldn't check out. He decided to take his bag to his car in the parking lot. That way he could stretch his legs before the journey.

He didn't pass anyone on the way to his car. After opening the hatchback, he tossed his bag inside. He started to set the book on top of it, but he stopped.

There was a bookmark inside it. Curious, Sam sat down on the bumper of his car and opened the book. He thumbed through it until he found the bookmarked page. Surprised, he saw that it was a book of poems. He hadn't read poetry since his high school English class. He hadn't been a fan then, and he doubted his tastes had changed much since. Still, Winnie had generously given him the book. She would never know if he didn't read it, but it felt rude not to.

He partially closed the book to see the author. It was no one he'd ever heard of. He shrugged. That didn't mean much. He couldn't name many poets off the top of his head.

Returning to the page that had been bookmarked, Sam saw that one of the poems had been highlighted. He usually cringed at writing or marks of any kind in a book. Now, however, he was much too curious about why he was supposed to read this poem to worry about it.

The poem described a man who had many things in his home. When a thief broke into his house and destroyed his belongings, the man didn't care. But the man fought back when the thief tried to damage the treasures he kept in his heart. The treasures were what the man valued. Without them, he was nothing.

Sam read the poem a second time, his heart thundering in his ears. Every word seemed directed at him, like an arrow hitting its target. His heart was the bull's-eye. Alyssa was his treasure. But unlike the man in the poem, Sam had stepped aside to let the thief steal his treasure.

If he left now, not only would his friendship with Alyssa be done, but he would also always wonder if they could have had a chance. He remembered Alyssa's expression that morning as he left her. She hadn't seemed like someone who was happy and in love with Justin. In fact, she hadn't looked happy at all. Was it possible that she didn't want to stay here with Justin?

No way was Sam leaving now. He closed the book, grabbed his bag, shut the hatchback door, and practically ran inside the inn.

Winnie was in the foyer talking to Grace.

Sam made a beeline for the older woman and shoved the poetry book into her hands. "I changed my mind. I'm not leaving." He dashed up the stairs.

Her sparkling laugh echoed behind him. He had a feeling she had known he would be hanging around a little longer.

He could still make it to the conference in time for lunch. Opening his door, he tossed his bag inside, then was off again. He hurried to the barn. When he entered, the attendees were forming a line at the buffet table.

Frantically, Sam glanced around until he spotted a sleek dark ponytail. He rushed over to Alyssa.

She stared at him, then grinned.

Sam hugged her tightly, and he felt her trembling. "Sorry I was in such a bad mood earlier. I decided that everything at home could wait."

"I'm glad." Alyssa bit her lip. "Would it be all right if I went home with you after the conference?"

"Absolutely. You know you can always join me."

"Thank you," she murmured, her tone dripping with relief.

As much as he hated to be the cause of her pain, it heartened him to know that she had felt their rift too. Surely that meant something.

"I thought you were going home," Justin said to Sam as he stepped beside Alyssa. "Important stuff to take care of."

"I changed my mind," Sam replied.

"Are you sure?" Justin asked.

Was that irritation in his voice? Sam ignored it. He was here to show Alyssa how much he loved her. But now wasn't the time. Maybe tomorrow during the Christmas party.

"I'm never too busy for the important things in life." Sam directed the comment to Justin, but he kept his gaze locked on Alyssa's. He was sure he saw a glimmer of understanding from her.

She gave a small smile, one meant just for him.

Sam realized he couldn't wait around and let Justin make the first move. "Tomorrow night's the Christmas party," he said to Alyssa. "Should we meet down in the foyer at five thirty?"

"That's a great plan." She grinned at him. "But the party starts at six. Are you saying five thirty because you know I'll be late?"

Sam chuckled. "I hadn't thought of that, but now that you mention it, maybe we should plan to meet at five. Then if you're late, we'll still be early."

"All right, let's meet around five," Alyssa said.

"I know when you say 'around' that you're already planning on being late." Sam rolled his eyes. It felt good, being able to tease her again. He had missed their easy relationship.

Sam and Alyssa laughed.

"I can meet you guys there," Justin said, "and the three of us can walk over together."

Sam and Alyssa both stopped laughing and turned to stare at Justin. His expression told Sam that Justin was serious. He was also quite sure that Justin knew he was stepping on Sam's toes, and he didn't care.

"There's no need for you to do that," Alyssa told Justin. "You're not staying at the inn, so it would make more sense for you to meet us here. Whoever arrives first can save seats."

Sam nodded.

"Nonsense," Justin said. "I'm going to be walking past the inn anyway. It would be fun to meet up with you two. That way we can be sure to get seats at the same table."

The only way to get out of sitting with Justin was to be rude, and Sam refused to sink to that level. He'd have to give in. He reminded himself that he still had a chance. He'd make sure that Justin didn't monopolize her time.

Someone called out to Justin.

Lifting his hand in a mock salute, Justin walked away from them.

Alyssa and Sam continued to the buffet line.

Sam took a deep breath. He was determined not to waste any more time. "I hope you'll save me a dance at the party." Inwardly he cringed. He sounded like a Jane Austen novel. Alyssa had made both him and Derek watch several Jane Austen movies when they were younger.

"Save you one?" She lifted an eyebrow. "If you don't dance with me, I'll be mad at you."

"Consider it done." He gave her a stiff little bow.

She chuckled and called him a dork.

Sam grinned. He might be a dork, but if he was her dork, he didn't care. He couldn't wait until the party tomorrow night.

Marcie

After Charles dropped off Savannah and left for his meeting, Marcie felt slightly anxious about her offer to babysit.

Marcie didn't have a lot of experience with children, but she'd always expected to get married and have kids someday. In high school, she'd gone through a phase when she bought wedding magazines and cut out dresses she liked and saved them in a binder. She'd dreamed about meeting the love of her life in college and getting married and starting a family by the time she was twenty-five. She had even created a list of possible names for her children.

But life hadn't worked out that way. She'd met Brian in college and fallen for him hard. He was handsome and funny. All her friends had a crush on him, and when he asked her on a date, she felt like she'd been handed the grand prize. Sometimes his humor was a little cruel, but she convinced herself that he was a good person and didn't really mean it.

They dated for five years before Brian proposed to her. She was feeling a little desperate by that point, so maybe that was why she'd accepted so quickly. Looking back, she could admit that she already had doubts about whether they were suited for each other.

Her best friend, Allie, couldn't stand Brian and wasn't shy about telling her so. "You can do so much better than him," Allie frequently said. "The way he treats you is not the way you're supposed to treat someone you love. It's almost disrespectful."

Allie was right. But by that time, Marcie had already invested five years of her life, and she didn't want to start over with someone else. She was thirty years old, and her dreams of having a family of her own were rapidly slipping away.

Marcie refused to make the mistake of pinning her hopes on a man again. She'd come to the realization that if she was going to be content, she needed to accept her life as it was. However, that didn't mean she was averse to anything happening between her and someone else in the future.

Savannah tapped Marcie's arm, then pointed to the door and made the sign for walk, followed by the sign for dog.

"I think you want to go find Winston," Marcie said. She knew that Savannah didn't understand her, so she repeated the sign for dog.

Savannah nodded.

They might as well search for Winston. She didn't have any toys for the girl to play with, only the ones that Charles had brought with them. Savannah hadn't been interested in any of them. It was going to be a long two hours if they didn't find something to do.

It didn't take long to locate Winston. As soon as they descended the stairs and entered the foyer, the dog trotted over to Savannah.

Savannah made cooing noises as she scratched Winston's belly.

The dog wagged his tail, soaking up the attention.

Marcie scanned the room and noticed Grace sitting behind the reception desk.

"Is there anything I can help you with?" the innkeeper asked.

"We're fine," Marcie said. "I'm watching Savannah for a couple of hours while Charles attends a meeting."

Grace's eyes lit with understanding. "That's right. Winnie couldn't watch her today. I'm glad you were able to step in."

"Me too," Marcie admitted as she glanced at the little girl. "It would make Savannah's day if she could take Winston for a walk."

"Of course," Grace said. "I'm sure Winston will enjoy it."

"Will he need a leash?" Marcie asked.

"If you stay on the grounds of the inn, he'll be fine," Grace said.

Marcie tapped Savannah on the shoulder to get her attention. "Dog. Walk." She held up her hands at shoulder level and shook them to show she was asking a question.

Immediately, Savannah stood.

Marcie's heart melted when Savannah took her hand. If Marcie and Charles did get together someday, she already knew that she would love his daughter. Savannah had easily woven her way into Marcie's heart.

It was beautiful outside. The sun was shining, and the temperature was mild. In Marcie's book, that was perfect weather for taking a walk.

Marcie and Savannah wandered the grounds with the dog. At one point, Marcie found a stick and handed it to Savannah so she could play fetch with Winston. The child shrieked with laughter every time the dog took off, his little legs pumping.

Savannah's laughter was contagious, and Marcie laughed so hard her stomach muscles started to ache. She didn't care. It felt good to be carefree and have something to chuckle about.

When they finally took Winston inside, they found Grace talking with Charlotte.

"How was your walk?" Grace asked.

"It was lovely," Marcie answered. "Thanks for letting Savannah play with Winston."

"Grace tells me that you and Savannah are on your own this afternoon," Charlotte said to Marcie. "Have you eaten lunch yet?"

Marcie shook her head.

"How would you and Savannah like to make something with me in the kitchen?" Charlotte asked.

"Are you sure you have time to do that?" Marcie didn't want to interfere with Charlotte's plans.

Charlotte grinned. "I always have time for cooking."

When Marcie told Savannah what they were going to do, the girl practically vibrated with excitement.

They followed Charlotte into her domain, and she helped them create individual pizzas. Savannah wanted pineapple and ham on hers. The confident way she picked those toppings made Marcie wonder if that was the way she ate pizza with her dad.

"I've never tried those toppings before," Marcie told Charlotte, sprinkling small pieces of ham onto her pizza. "I guess today's as good a time as any."

While they waited for their pizzas to bake, Charlotte let Savannah help her prepare chocolate mousse for hospitality hour. Savannah seemed to enjoy being Charlotte's assistant.

When the timer dinged, Charlotte removed the pizzas from the oven and cut them. She transferred the slices to plates and set them on the island along with glasses of lemonade and napkins. "Let's dig in."

To her surprise, Marcie liked the mixture of the tangy red sauce and the sweet pineapple. It wasn't her favorite kind of pizza, but she'd definitely eat it again. "Good," she signed to Savannah.

The little girl smiled.

They had just finished their lunch when Charles returned.

Savannah ran to her dad, squealing when he picked her up and threw her into the air as if she weighed nothing. He set her down, and they signed a brief conversation.

Marcie didn't catch everything, but she knew that Savannah told him about Winston and baking her own pizza.

"She said she had a good time," Charles told Marcie. "Did you have any problems?"

"No problems," Marcie answered. "We walked the dog, played fetch, and Savannah introduced me to the joys of eating pineapple on my pizza. All and all, I would say it's been an exceptional day." She smiled at Savannah and signed, "Fun day."

Savannah nodded.

After thanking Charlotte for lunch, Marcie, Charles, and Savannah left the kitchen. Without discussing it, they headed toward the front door. It was too nice a day to stay inside.

Winston appeared out of nowhere and followed them outside.

Savannah and Winston played in the yard while Marcie and Charles watched them from the rockers on the porch.

"How was your meeting?" Marcie asked.

"It was fine," Charles replied. "Like I said, I met with a current customer. He was satisfied with our services, so it was an easy meeting." He smiled. "I brought you some pie from Aunt Patsy's Porch."

She grinned. "What kind?"

"It's a whole pie," he said. "I thought the three of us could share it. It's mixed berry. Is that okay?"

"Please," Marcie scoffed. "I love almost every kind of pie."

"Even though I forgot the ice cream?" Charles asked.

She placed her hand on her chest and stared at him as if horrified. "No ice cream? That's terrible."

"I know. Unforgivable."

Marcie chuckled. "Seriously, I'll eat pie with or without ice cream. It's all good."

"I left it in my room," he said. "I'll be right back."

As Marcie waited for Charles, she reflected on what a thoughtful man he was. Once again, she hoped that they would be able to stay in touch.

Charles returned with a large tray. "Charlotte gave me forks, plates, and napkins. And she insisted on bottles of water."

They sat under a large shady tree to eat their slices of pie.

When they were done, Marcie used a few napkins to clean Savannah's face. "She'll have to use soap and water when you get inside."

"What's a little mess to a kid?" Charles asked. "Part of the joy of childhood is being able to get dirty."

Savannah stretched out under the tree, and Winston curled up beside her. The pair was asleep within five minutes.

"You really wore her out," he commented. "I haven't been able to get her to take a nap in a long time."

She smiled. "Guilty."

They sat in companionable silence for a few minutes. Marcie was more content than she'd been in years.

"Excuse me. My phone's ringing." Charles reached into his pocket and took out his phone. When he checked the screen, he frowned. "What do you want, Kelly?"

Marcie watched Charles as he spoke on the phone. Clearly, this call wasn't expected or wanted. Who was Kelly? She'd never heard him mention the name before.

"Hang on a second," Charles told Kelly. He turned to Marcie. "I'm sorry, but this call is important."

"I understand." She wanted to do something to help because he appeared worried. "I'll take Savannah to my room, and you can get her when you're done."

"Thank you," he said. "I'll be there as soon as I can."

She gently awoke Savannah. The sleepy child stumbled to her feet. When she leaned heavily against Marcie's side, Marcie bent and picked her up. She wasn't that heavy. Marcie settled her on her hip, and Savannah dropped her head onto Marcie's shoulder. Savannah's soft breathing tickled her neck.

Winston followed Marcie as she carried Savannah to the inn. When they entered, the dog trotted toward the kitchen.

Marcie climbed the stairs to the second floor. Sweat was beading on her upper lip by the time they reached her room. She settled the child on her bed, then sat in a chair to wait. She tried to read a book, but it was difficult to focus.

It was almost forty-five minutes later when she received a text from Charles. *I'm standing outside your room.*

After setting her book down, she opened the door.

He walked inside, glancing at Savannah asleep on the bed. His mouth was set, angry. "That was Kelly, my wife's younger sister."

Marcie studied him. The pallor of his skin and the despair in his eyes worried her. Something was dreadfully wrong. "What did she want?" It didn't take a genius to guess she had called because of his daughter.

"She wanted to warn me." Charles ran a hand through his hair. The disheveled look made his tension and despair more obvious.

"Warn you?" she repeated. She crossed her arms to keep from shivering.

He motioned to the veranda. They walked outside, and she took a seat.

Charles paced for a few moments before shoving his hands into his pockets and leaning against the railing. "Kelly's parents are moving forward with their plan to take Savannah from me. They hired a lawyer, and they're talking about getting a private investigator. They intend to show that I'm neglecting Savannah's needs."

Appalled wasn't a strong enough word to describe her feelings. The man in front of her was a loving and attentive father. It was beyond despicable for Savannah's grandparents to do this to him. The air of despair emanating from him was nearly tangible. She wanted to walk over and hug him, but she resisted. He needed logic right now. Actually, he needed a lawyer.

"Why did Kelly warn you?" Marcie asked.

He stared at her. "What?"

"I'm assuming that she disagrees with her parents' actions," she said. "Her calling you suggests that she's on your side with this. If the case goes to court, would she be willing to risk her parents' wrath to testify on your behalf?"

Charles blinked at her, and hope glimmered on his face.

Marcie was glad to see that he hadn't given up.

His expression took on a thoughtful quality. "She might be willing to testify. I know there's been tension between Kelly and her parents. As medieval as it sounds, Louis paid her fiancé to go away."

"That's rough." The more she heard about this couple, the more she disliked them. "Why would he do something like that?"

"Apparently, Kelly's choice of a husband wasn't any more appropriate or acceptable than Joanna's was."

Marcie's mind whirled with all the threads. "We might be able to use that in your case. Do you have any negative or threatening letters, e-mails, or anything else that will help us prove they're harassing you?"

Charles nodded. "I have all of that."

She gave him a tight smile. "Well, that's good news for you. People tend to forget that once you put something out there electronically, it doesn't go away. Even if he cleaned out his hard drive or destroyed his phone and bought a new one, you still have the evidence. And that data is retrievable even if he erased it."

"So he sent me some nasty messages," he said. "How does that help me? After all, just because he's cruel doesn't mean that I'm fit to be a father."

"True," Marcie said. "However, it muddies the waters. If we can prove that he's underhanded, a jury or a judge will be less likely to believe him. And it'll draw into question whether he is more fit to be Savannah's guardian than you are."

"What do you mean by 'we'?" Charles asked. "I think we're friends, but this isn't your concern."

She didn't let his words bother her. She knew what he was saying. Lifting her chin, she said, "You need a lawyer. I'm still a lawyer. Not to brag, but I'm very good. I have an impressive track record."

"I don't know if I can let you do that. You weren't sure you wanted to practice law anymore. Wouldn't helping me put you right back where you didn't want to be?"

Marcie was touched that he was taking her feelings into consideration, but it wasn't necessary. In that moment, everything was crystal-clear to her. "I'm not backing down from this. And you're wrong. I do know what I want."

He didn't say anything.

She stood and walked toward him. "Your in-laws are trying to force you to change who Savannah is because they're not comfortable. They don't care if she's happy and healthy. Being deaf is not a disease. It's a huge part of who Savannah is. I want to represent you."

Charles watched her carefully. "If you assist us, then whatever is happening between us can't go any farther until it's all settled."

She felt a tingle of joy when he acknowledged the chemistry brewing between them. But he was right. Now was not the time. "Agreed. We can't have a conflict of interest. Right now, I want to help, and more than that, I'm confident that I can help you."

When he gazed into her eyes again, hope and determination blazed from their depths. "Let's do this. Help me keep my daughter."

23

Charles

Charles got up early Friday morning. He'd slept restlessly, replaying his conversations with Marcie and Kelly the day before. The situation with his in-laws worried him more than he cared to admit.

Louis had hired a lawyer and possibly a private detective. Charles shook his head, unable to believe Joanna had been born to such vile people. His wife had been honest to a fault, and she had never said or done anything to hurt another soul.

Probably because she had been hurt by her own family. Charles cringed. Those were the people who wanted to raise Savannah. He glanced at his daughter, still sleeping peacefully. He refused to let them take her away.

Charles recalled first meeting Joanna's younger sister, Kelly. She was full of anger, and he could tell that she was always on the verge of unleashing her vitriol on anyone who crossed her. He had avoided her at all costs.

But Kelly had softened around Joanna, and once in a while, she would be kind to her older sister. Charles had never seen Kelly treat anyone else in such a gentle manner.

Soon after Charles and Joanna got married, Kelly had disappeared. Charles knew that Joanna had worried about her sister, even though she hadn't talked about her much. He had thought it was odd that Joanna's parents hadn't talked about Kelly either.

No one heard anything from Kelly until she suddenly returned months later.

Kelly had explained to Joanna what had happened. She had fallen in love with an adjunct college professor. She never did tell Joanna his name. They had dated quietly for a few months. When he asked her to marry him, she remembered the nasty comments that Joanna had heard about Charles from their parents. Her father had demanded that Joanna give him up, but Joanna had shocked him by standing her ground. Charles had not known how much pressure she had been under until years later.

Kelly had begged her fiancé to elope, like Joanna and Charles had done. He had argued that it was unfair. She was a young woman, and she should have the wedding of her dreams. Kelly had given in. They had told her parents that they were going to be married. But Louis had set up a secret meeting with the fiancé and offered to buy him off. The man had taken the money and left town. Kelly had been heartbroken.

Kelly's mother had recently attempted to reconcile with her daughter, and Kelly had found out that her father had hired a lawyer to get custody of Savannah.

Kelly had gone out of her way to warn Charles about it. He couldn't see how it was a trap.

Charles need to thank Kelly, and he wanted to ask her about testifying for him. He decided to give her a call.

Kelly answered on the second ring. "Good morning."

"First off, I want to thank you for the warning yesterday," Charles said.

"You're welcome," she replied. "I did it for Joanna."

"I realize that, but I still appreciate the heads-up." He drew in a deep breath. "I have a question for you. I hired an attorney yesterday, and she wants to know if you would be willing to testify in court in my defense."

"I'm not sure," Kelly admitted. "I'll have to consider it."

It wasn't the answer he was hoping for, but at least she hadn't flat-out refused. "If you agree to do it, you'll probably have to answer questions that put your parents in a poor light."

"My father should never be in charge of any child again," she stated. "Your daughter should not have to endure what Joanna and I did."

"Savannah is my entire world," Charles said. "I'll do everything I can to keep her safe, healthy, and happy."

"I know you will," Kelly said. "I can give you the name of the lawyer he hired. If you want to, you can ask him to meet with my parents and your lawyer."

"I would appreciate it."

Kelly relayed the name of the attorney and his phone number, and Charles jotted them down in his notebook.

"Go ahead and tell your lawyer that I will testify against my father," she said, her voice quivering.

Surprised, he asked, "Why are you doing this?"

"He bullied me and Joanna," Kelly said. "He separated me from the man I was going to marry, and I know he tried to do the same to you and Joanna. Savannah should not have to deal with his cruelty. She should have the opportunity to make her own decisions in life."

"I can't thank you enough," Charles said. His spirits rose. It felt good to know that he had someone else in his corner.

After he hung up with Kelly, he started to dial the attorney's number, but he ended up setting down the phone before he made the call. As a business owner, he knew the value of caution and thinking things through. Before he made any moves, he needed to speak with Marcie. If she advised him to set up the meeting with the lawyer, he would proceed.

Checking his watch, he realized they had less than an hour before they were supposed to meet Marcie for breakfast. He woke Savannah and encouraged her to get ready quickly. It was not easy. His daughter had been born stubborn. If she didn't want to move, it took a lot of wheedling and bargaining to change her mind. Today was one of those days.

They were ten minutes late meeting Marcie in the dining room. She sat at the table with Alyssa, Sam, Howard, and Wanda. They were already eating.

Charles guided Savannah to the buffet table. He helped her choose toast, scrambled eggs, and orange juice. He selected an omelet, bacon, and a cup of coffee for himself.

"Let me take that for you," Grace offered. She carried Savannah's plate and juice to the table.

"Thanks," Charles said. He ushered his daughter to a seat at the table and sat down beside her. Marcie was on his other side, and he apologized for being late.

Sam grinned at Savannah, and Alyssa signed good morning to her. The little girl was delighted.

Grace and Charlotte both repeated the signs to Savannah. She bounced in her seat with excitement.

"You've been busy," Charles murmured to Marcie.

She grinned. "While I was waiting for you, I decided to teach the others a few signs myself."

Charles had always thought the phrase *dancing eyes* was ridiculous. But when he gazed at Marcie, he realized her eyes were definitely dancing. And it was at his expense. It was even more surprising to find that he didn't mind one bit.

What was it about this woman that brought him out of his dark moods? He'd been so sure that he'd have nothing to smile about today, and here he was fighting a grin within minutes of joining her.

Marcie O'Connor was a special woman.

"I called Kelly this morning. She agreed to testify against her father."

Charles took a sip of his coffee while he waited for Marcie's reaction.

"Perfect. That alone might be enough to get your father-in-law to back off. Having an insider spill your secrets is bad for business. His reputation might never recover."

"She also gave me the phone number for the lawyer my father-in-law hired," he added.

Marcie smiled. It wasn't her normal friendly one. It was smug. "If it's okay with you, I'm going to e-mail my boss. He can schedule a meeting."

"It's fine with me," Charles said.

She pulled out her tablet and tapped out an e-mail.

While he waited, he finished his breakfast.

When Marcie was done, she turned her tablet toward him. "What do you think?"

As Charles read the message, he was glad that he'd hired Marcie. "That might be enough to make Louis think twice. Not only do I have a lawyer, but you're familiar with the advocacy issues for the deaf and hard of hearing. It sounds fierce."

She had also included comments about due process cases and legal battles with individuals with hearing loss. And she had put it together in the time it had taken him to eat an omelet and bacon. He was impressed.

"Here goes," Marcie said, sending the message. She set her tablet aside. "Do you have any more meetings today?"

"No, today is all about playing tourist with my daughter." Charles hesitated, then plunged ahead. "I know we want to be careful about conflicts of interest, but I'd like you to join us as a friend."

Marcie nodded. "I'd like that. Even if we weren't working on this case, I need to clean up the mess I've made of my life before I can think of getting into any kind of relationship."

He realized something. "You're better at lipreading than you were a few days ago."

She shrugged. "I practiced the skill all through high school, so it's not new to me. I've been a little rusty lately because I've never needed to rely on it completely before."

"Savannah doesn't wear hearing aids," Charles said. "She didn't get any benefit from them. I hope this isn't an offensive question, but have you tried them?"

"I have. They didn't work for me either."

He let the subject drop.

Her phone lit up with an e-mail. Marcie read it and smiled. "My boss is going to contact the lawyer right away. He likes my angle on it, and he welcomed me back to work. Apparently, he doesn't agree with Brian that I should be fired."

"That's great news, but I hope working with Brian won't be a problem."

"It won't be for me," she said. "I'm over him completely. If he has an issue, then he'll have to figure it out. He can't make me leave."

Charles was glad to see her so optimistic.

Her phone lit up again. This time when Marcie read the e-mail, her eyes widened. "My boss told me that Brian is no longer with the firm. No explanation." She glanced at Charles. "I'll bet they fired him for taking notes about me. That could be considered discrimination."

"I'm glad you won't have to work with him anymore," he said.

"Me too." She stared down at her empty plate.

Charles could tell that the conversation was upsetting her, so he changed the subject. "What would you like to do today?"

"I'm not sure," Marcie said.

The other guests had already left the dining room for the last day of the conference, and Grace was clearing the empty dishes from the table. "I don't mean to interrupt, but can I make a suggestion?"

"Yes, please," Charles said.

"There's a wonderful arts center in downtown Magnolia Harbor," Grace said. "They have a hands-on section for children. Savannah might enjoy it."

Charles signed to his daughter.

Savannah excitedly signed back, telling him she wanted to go.

"Savannah's all for it," Charles said, then faced Marcie. "Are you game?"

"I don't know much about art," she said, "but I would love to learn."

Grace gave them directions to the Dorothy A. Prescott Arts Center, and they piled into Charles's car. Soon they arrived at the impressive brick building with large windows.

As they exited the car, they noticed a sculpture garden on one side of the building. They strolled around the garden. Savannah seemed to be in awe as she studied the magnificent pieces.

When they had seen all the sculptures, they headed to the main entrance. Charles held the door open for Marcie and Savannah. The spacious lobby was two stories high, with balconies ringing the second floor. Paintings, pottery, and sculptures were prominently displayed.

A young woman with long dark hair greeted them from behind a tall counter. "Welcome to the arts center. I'm Brianna Lawrence. How can I help you?"

"My daughter is interested in the hands-on children's section," Charles said, then explained that Savannah was deaf.

"I know a few signs." Brianna signed a greeting to Savannah. She opened a half door and came out from behind the counter. "Follow me."

They followed Brianna down a corridor lined with classrooms

and artwork on the walls. She stopped and opened one of the doors. "Here it is."

Savannah gaped at the colorful room and all the different art stations.

"What would you like to do first?" Charles signed to his daughter.

Savannah made a beeline for the painting section, then motioned for Charles and Marcie to join her.

Brianna showed them the supplies and demonstrated a couple of painting techniques, and Savannah got to work. Soon she persuaded Charles and Marcie to paint their own pictures with her.

Charles was surprised by how much he enjoyed it. Savannah enthusiastically worked on her painting, and he joked with Marcie about his own disastrous efforts. As Marcie laughed and teased him, the anxiety he'd been feeling began to melt away.

They thanked Brianna and left the arts center. Savannah clutched her painting as they walked to the car.

It was lunchtime, so they stopped at Cappy's for pizza. Savannah could barely eat her food. All she wanted to do was talk about how much fun she'd had. Charles was pleased to see her so excited.

During lunch Louis called Charles. His father-in-law began ranting and raving, and Charles declined to speak with him, because he needed his lawyer's counsel.

Marcie gave him a thumbs-up from across the table.

Louis was still yelling when Charles hung up the phone.

"Good grief," Marcie said, checking her phone. "My boss e-mailed me again. Your in-laws are insisting on meeting you today to discuss this."

"Unless it's a video call, it will have to wait until I get home," Charles said. "He started this, and I refuse to accommodate him any more than I already have."

"I'll tell him." She sent the message.

Soon a video conference was set up for later that afternoon. Marcie's boss agreed to sit in and represent Charles, because she didn't think she would be able to see them well enough to read their lips. Charles called Kelly, and she offered to join the meeting even on such short notice.

In the meantime, they went to the movies. There was a new princess film Savannah wanted to see.

Charles bought them a large bucket of buttery popcorn to share, and Marcie rented a portable device that provided closed-captioning so she could watch the movie and read the words.

They selected seats in the nearly empty theater. When the film started, Savannah was mesmerized by the animation. It didn't matter that she couldn't hear it.

Charles was filled with dread about the video conference, but when he glanced at his smiling daughter, he felt a sense of peace.

With Marcie's help, he would fight with everything he had to keep Savannah where she belonged.

24

Grace

When Grace entered the kitchen that afternoon, she found Charlotte and Dean sitting at the island with cups of coffee and toffee bars.

"Charlotte told me the big news." Dean got up and gave Grace a hug. "Congratulations."

"Thank you," Grace said. "I still can't believe it."

"Have a seat." Charlotte patted the stool next to her. "Try these toffee bars Dean brought over."

"You don't have to twist my arm," Grace said with a grin. She sat down and sampled one of the treats. "It's amazing."

"You need to give me the recipe," Charlotte said to Dean. "I'd like to make them for hospitality hour."

"Are you kidding?" he joked. "I can't give away my secrets."

Charlotte playfully swatted his arm.

"I hate to run, but I have to get back to The Tidewater." Dean kissed Charlotte on the cheek, then turned to Grace. "I'm so happy for you and Spencer. I know Charlotte's already planning the food, but let me know if I can help too."

"I really appreciate it," Grace said. "I'll keep you posted."

"Enjoy the rest of the toffee bars," Dean said, then walked out the back door.

Charlotte refilled her cup of coffee. "So you're breaking the news to the kids tonight. Are you excited?"

"I certainly am."

"I'm sure they'll be thrilled," Charlotte said. "Soon we'll all be one big happy family."

"And Christmas will be even more special this year." Grace smiled as she pictured everyone gathered for the holidays. She couldn't imagine a more joyous occasion. "I can hardly wait."

Charles

When they returned to the inn, it was almost time for the video conference. Marcie took Savannah outside to play with Winston while Charles went to his room.

The meeting was brutal. Charles almost felt bad for Louis's lawyer. The man was doing his job, but several times he appeared as shocked as everyone else by the hate spewing from Louis's mouth. No matter how many times the lawyer told him to hold his peace, Louis kept talking.

As Kelly talked about her father's controlling habits while she was growing up, Charles shuddered. She had spoken the truth when she said no child should be in his care.

Louis began to argue.

But his lawyer stopped him and addressed Charles. "One reason we're here is that Louis and Margaret believe you are neglecting your daughter. They claim that you are isolating her emotionally from her family and peers."

Charles was furious. He paused to regain control of himself. "Savannah has not been neglected. She is loved, and she is a well-adjusted child. Their actual problem is that she's deaf. She was born deaf. After considering all the options, my late wife and I decided that it would be best if Savannah was raised using American Sign Language. She goes to school, she has friends, and she is beginning to read. The only thing she doesn't do is hear."

"That's not the only thing," Louis snapped. "My granddaughter doesn't speak a word."

Suddenly, Charles had had enough dancing around the subject. "Savannah talks in sign language all day long. She doesn't speak, but that's fine. You want her to go through a surgery that neither her mother nor I wanted. As I've told you before, if Savannah decides she wants a cochlear implant when she's older, I will revisit the subject. It will be her decision. Until then, she's a happy child, and all her needs are being met."

"My granddaughter—"

"Savannah," Charles practically growled. "Why is it that Savannah is almost six years old and I have never once heard you say her name?"

Ten seconds of silence followed that remark.

"You've never said her name?" Marcie's boss asked, incredulous. Louis ignored him.

So did his lawyer. "Mr. Johnston, I understand that you have hired an advocate?"

Charles smiled. "Yes, I have hired an advocate who is especially knowledgeable about the laws regarding special education and people who are deaf and hard of hearing. I'm assuming that you are familiar with deaf culture and advocates for the deaf and hard of hearing?"

The lawyer pursed his lips. "I would like to confer with my client for a few minutes." He muted the call.

As Charles watched Louis, he could see the fury blooming on his face. Whatever the lawyer said to him, he obviously didn't like it.

Charles heard someone entering the room. He turned to see Marcie standing to the side, holding Savannah's hand. They were both out of the camera's range.

Charles muted their side of the conversation.

Marcie narrowed her eyes as she stared at the monitor. "It appears that your father-in-law is arguing with his attorney."

Charles glanced at the screen. She was right. Louis was definitely arguing with his lawyer. If the situation wasn't so serious, it would have been rather comical.

"Winnie invited Savannah and me to her house for ice cream," Marcie said. "Would it be all right with you if we went?"

"Of course. After I finish here, I'll drive over and join you."

"See you soon." She left with Savannah.

He waited for Louis and his attorney to end their little conference. Another five minutes passed before the microphone was unmuted.

"I have conferred with my client," the lawyer said. "In light of the information provided here, my client is withdrawing any attempt to seek custody of Savannah Johnston."

The breath he'd been holding exploded from Charles. It was over. His in-laws had backed down, exactly as Marcie had predicted. He could hardly believe it. Louis never backed down from a fight.

As he disconnected the call, his heart was so light that it felt like a feather in his chest. He took the stairs two at a time, humming under his breath. Which amused him. His family always said he couldn't carry a note in a bucket.

He didn't care.

He got into his car and drove the short distance to Winnie's house. He jogged to the front door and knocked.

"Come in!"

Hearing Winnie's cheerful invitation, he opened the door and followed the sound of clinking spoons until he found them in the kitchen.

Marcie stood and walked to him. "What happened?"

Charles couldn't resist. He picked her up and swung her around in a circle.

"Put me down!" Marcie shrieked, holding on tight. "Oh, my goodness. I'm going to be dizzy."

He set her on her feet. She was swaying, but she was also laughing.

"I take it you have good news," Winnie said with a grin.

"I have the best news, thanks to my brilliant lawyer." Charles gestured to Marcie. "At the advice of his attorney, my father-in-law has given up his case to take custody of Savannah."

"I think I'd like to meet your lawyer one day," Marcie quipped.

He glanced at her. "I do think you're brilliant, you know. Brilliant, amazing, and beautiful."

Her cheeks were as red as a stop sign. Her eyes, though, were luminous.

"I think you're pretty amazing yourself," she whispered.

Charles smiled at Marcie, then went over and hugged Savannah. He felt a tremendous sense of relief now that he didn't need to worry about anyone taking her away from him. As he held her close, he was overcome with gratitude for his precious daughter. And for the wonderful woman who had ensured that Savannah would stay with him.

26

Sam

Sam hurried down to the foyer at 4:50. He wanted to be waiting for Alyssa before Justin showed up to walk with them to the party. It was unlikely that she would arrive early or even on time, but he wasn't going to take any chances.

At 4:55, Alyssa flowed down the stairs, her emerald-green dress swishing around her calves as she moved. Her dark curls had been pinned in an elaborate manner on her head. One curl had been left to brush the side of her neck. Her eyes seemed to be lit from within and sparkled like gems.

His breath stalled in his chest, and it took a moment to remember how to breathe. Alyssa was magnificent. There was no other way to describe her.

"You're amazing," Sam said, no longer trying to disguise how he felt about her. Tonight he planned to lay it all out on the line. If she rejected him, at least he'd know. But he'd probably have to quit his job and move.

"You look good too," Alyssa commented, motioning to his dark-gray suit. "I don't see you dressed up very often."

"When we get home, maybe we should dress up and go out somewhere," he suggested.

She stilled, searching his face. "Are you flirting with me?"

"Most definitely."

"I—"

"Hey, you guys are both here," Justin interrupted from behind him. "Wow, Alyssa, you're gorgeous."

Annoyance flashed over Alyssa's face, but she didn't say anything.

Sam knew she'd been irritated by Justin's arrival. He could work with that. With no other choice, he greeted Justin.

The three of them headed to the barn. The sound of Christmas carols could be heard as soon as they entered.

Sam scanned the food tables. One featured hors d'oeuvres, such as cheese and crackers, sliced fruit and veggies, and an assortment of dips. Another table offered more than a dozen different types of Christmas cookies. On the last table, a chocolate fountain gurgled, and strawberries, oranges, and pretzels were available for dipping.

"I'll be full before they get around to serving dinner," Sam remarked.

"I might just pull up a chair at the cookie table," Alyssa said.

"Not the chocolate fountain?" Sam teased.

She shook her head. "It might splatter on my dress."

They kept up a steady stream of remarks as they walked to the table with drinks. Oddly, Justin didn't join the conversation. Sam wondered briefly what was going on, but he didn't dwell on it.

Sam poured two glasses of punch, then handed one to Alyssa.

After Justin took a glass, he said, "Let's go find a table."

"There are a few seats at that one." Alyssa pointed to a table close to the band.

Sam noticed that Howard and Wanda were sitting there. He motioned for Alyssa to lead the way.

Justin glanced in the direction she was heading. His lip curled slightly, but he didn't comment as he followed.

"I hope you guys are enjoying the party," Sam said to Howard and Wanda. "Are these seats taken?"

"Please join us," Howard responded. He sounded relieved. "We're not saving them."

"That is a stunning dress," Wanda said to Alyssa. "Have we met before?"

Nothing in Alyssa's expression gave away that she'd talked with Wanda several times. "Thank you. I'm Alyssa, and they're Sam and Justin."

Wanda greeted the men.

Howard squeezed his wife's hand. His gaze held a mixture of sadness and pure adoration.

Sam soon got the impression that the Wanda they were talking to tonight was the real Wanda. She was sweet and had a delightful sense of irony. Before long, their table was the loudest because they were all laughing so hard.

For the first time since the conference began, Justin didn't dominate the conversation or try to one-up everyone else. He seemed distracted this evening, but he did participate.

When the caterers began serving the entrées, everyone took their seats. Tonight there would be no speakers, no work. It was all about socializing and getting to know other professionals who worked in the same field around the country.

They continued their lively conversation over their dinner of roast beef, scalloped potatoes, maple-glazed carrots, and buttered rolls.

"I'm stuffed," Sam remarked as he pushed his empty plate aside. "But everything was so good."

"Does that mean you won't get me some cookies?" Alyssa asked, batting her eyelashes at him.

Sam narrowed his eyes. He suspected that she knew how adorable she was. "You're not playing fair."

Alyssa batted her lashes again.

Everyone at the table laughed.

"You win," Sam said with a dramatic sigh. "I'll get you a few cookies. But you'll have to share."

"Of course," Alyssa responded. "That goes without saying."

Sam left the table and strode over to the desserts. He selected several cookies and arranged them neatly on a plate. When he returned to the table, the dancing had started. Justin was leading Alyssa on to the dance floor. He frowned. How had he missed his opportunity already?

It wouldn't happen again. When this song was over, he'd ask her for a dance.

Sam sat down and watched the couples. Most of them swayed to the slow song, but Howard and Wanda stole the show with a series of complicated steps. When the tempo changed, the couple slid effortlessly into a graceful foxtrot. Many of the couples moved out of the way until there was a circle around Howard and Wanda.

When the song ended, applause broke out.

Howard bowed, and Wanda curtsied.

Sam recalled a previous conversation with Howard. The man had said that he didn't regret marrying Wanda, and some things in life were worth the risk. As the couple danced to the next song, Sam could see a lifetime of memories connecting them.

Alyssa was coming toward Sam, and Justin was behind her. Sam recognized this was his chance. Before Justin could ask Alyssa for a second dance, Sam pushed through the crowd toward her.

"May I have this dance?" he asked, his voice devoid of all humor. He held out his arm.

Alyssa took his arm, and Sam escorted her to the dance floor. She put her arms around his neck, and it seemed like the most natural thing in the world. For those few minutes as they swayed to the music, he stopped thinking and simply basked in her presence.

When the song ended, Alyssa dropped her arms from around his neck.

Sam was afraid she would rush back to the table, so before she had the chance, he asked, "Want to take a stroll outside?"

She held his gaze for a moment, then nodded.

Sam guided her outside, ushering her away from the people milling around. He stopped and faced her. Suddenly, his words dried up. The temptation to hold his tongue was strong, but his need to admit the truth was stronger. "Alyssa . . ."

"Yes?"

Sam realized he didn't know how to broach the subject. Flustered, he blurted, "I love you."

Alyssa didn't respond.

"I've loved you since high school, possibly even longer," he continued. "I wasn't going to say anything before. I know how much you loved Derek, and I didn't want to destroy our friendship. But when I saw that you weren't wearing your wedding rings, I decided to take a chance and tell you."

"You really love me?" Alyssa asked.

"Yes, I do," Sam said, feeling a rush of emotion. "I love the way you laugh and tease. I love how intelligent and caring you are." He grinned. "I even love how competitive you get when we're playing games or watching football."

Alyssa stared at the ground. "You're the reason I decided to remove my wedding rings. When I first realized several months ago that I'd developed feelings for you, I felt guilty. Like I had betrayed Derek. But as time went on, I remembered how close you and Derek were. I thought that maybe it would be all right. Derek wouldn't want me sitting at home moping for the rest of my life."

His heart soared. She felt the same way. "No, he wouldn't. When we first arrived, I really felt like we had a connection. I thought there was a chance. But then Justin happened."

"I wasn't interested in Justin," she scoffed.

"But you were thinking of letting him drive you home," Sam reminded her.

"Not really. I mentioned it, hoping that you would mind, but instead you said you were leaving early and told me to be happy."

He smiled in the dark. "I knew that comment would come back to haunt me. The only reason I was leaving was because I felt like I had lost my chance with you. But the more I thought about it, the more I realized that you are what I treasure most. So, I decided to stay and fight for you."

"That's so medieval yet romantic."

"I thought you'd like it."

They laughed.

"Was it hard seeing me married to Derek?" Alyssa asked as they started walking again.

"I don't know how to answer that," he replied honestly. "Of course it was hard. But at the same time, I was glad to see the two people I loved more than anything in the world together. It made it easier for me to watch you with him. I could stand you not being with me as long as you were happy."

She shivered.

"Want to go back inside?" Sam asked, putting his arm around her.

"Sure," Alyssa said. "I didn't get the cookies you promised."

He laughed.

When they returned to the barn, another slow song was playing.

Sam and Alyssa moved onto the dance floor. No one existed in that moment except for her. As they stood together in the middle of room, Sam leaned down and did what he'd dreamed of doing for seventeen years. Sam Matthews kissed Alyssa Larson.

By the time they went to their table for the plate of cookies, Justin had already left.

Grace

With Winston on her heels, Grace hurried to her quarters to get ready for dinner with Spencer and their children.

This was becoming a habit. It was the third dinner with Spencer this week. She smiled. In fact, soon she'd be seeing him for dinner every night.

Grace hugged herself with the sheer delight of it, then held out her left hand, moving it so she could view the ring from various angles. It sparkled where the light touched it. Spencer had done a fabulous job picking out this stunning engagement ring. She loved it.

Realizing she was woolgathering, she finished getting dressed. Grace was excited to see Spencer's daughters. She really liked them, and she was so pleased to be joining the family.

When she was ready, she stopped by the kitchen to say goodbye to Charlotte. "Winston and I are heading to Spencer's. Jake is meeting us there."

"Have a wonderful time." Charlotte smiled. "Tell Jake I'm making his favorite dishes tomorrow."

"I will. Thanks." Grace and Winston left the inn and walked to her car. It was a short drive to Spencer's house.

Spencer and Bailey greeted them at the door. Spencer gave Grace a hug while the dogs sniffed each other.

"You look beautiful," he commented.

"Thank you." She admired her ring again. "I keep trying to convince myself that it's real."

"It's real," Spencer assured her. "But I know what you mean. When you wanted to put a halt on our relationship earlier in the year, I was scared I would lose you. Now that you've agreed to marry me, I feel more relaxed than I've felt in a long time."

Grace laughed. "You always seem relaxed to me."

"What can I say? I'm a good actor." He caught her hand. "So you like the ring? I was worried that I should have let you pick it out."

"It's absolutely perfect," she responded. "I would have chosen the same one."

"I'm so relieved you like it."

"Can I help you with dinner?" Grace asked.

"It's almost ready," Spencer said. "I made spaghetti and meatballs and garlic bread."

"Sounds great," she said as she followed him into the kitchen.

It felt so right, working together in the kitchen. They talked and laughed as they put the finishing touches on the meal.

Grace was setting the table when she heard a car pull into the driveway. Bailey barked and bounded to the door.

On impulse, Grace snatched her ring off her finger.

"Why did you take it off?" Spencer asked, raising his eyebrows.

"Because if the kids see the ring right away, they'll know we're engaged," she explained. "I want us to tell them."

He hugged her shoulders. "If that's the way you want it, then it's fine with me." He left the room.

Grace heard Spencer talking with his daughters as they entered the house.

Bailey's barking dwindled to yips and whining. She was evidently getting spoiled with attention. Winston probably was too.

Grace smiled at Kylie and Megan as they walked into the dining room.

Their return smiles were tight and almost cold.

Grace shivered, though the house was warm. Something was going on, and she didn't like it.

Kylie helped set the table. In fact, she practically took over. It was almost as if she resented Grace doing the simple chore.

Grace pivoted to see Spencer standing in the doorway. His expression was blank as he watched his daughters. She wasn't imagining it. Spencer felt it too.

Another car pulled into the driveway. Grace was relieved that Jake was here. She went to greet him, and the dogs beat her to the door.

"I'm so glad to see you," she said, giving her son a hug. "Thanks for coming."

"No problem," Jake said, sounding wary. He averted his eyes as he petted the dogs.

Grace's confusion grew. First, Spencer's daughters were acting strangely and now Jake. "Let's go inside. Dinner's almost ready." She led her son into the house, and the dogs followed.

"Good to see you," Spencer said to Jake.

"You too," Jake said, then greeted Kylie and Megan.

"Why don't you all sit down so we can start?" Spencer asked. "I'll get the food."

Everyone took their seats, and Spencer went to the kitchen. He returned with a platter of spaghetti and meatballs. After passing it to Megan, he sat down.

"I don't know how much I'll be able to eat," Megan said. Her voice had an uncharacteristic bite to it. "I don't have much of an appetite today."

Spencer's daughters exchanged glances.

Grace's stomach knotted. Kylie and Megan knew something was going on, and they were upset about it. She tried to convince herself it was a mistake. They'd be fine once they heard the news. She brushed her hand against her pocket and felt the ring inside. The joy she'd felt ever since Spencer proposed suddenly turned to ashes in her mouth.

Grace noticed that Spencer had lost a little color. She hated seeing him so stressed, and she wished she could do something to ease his worry.

As if sensing her anxiety, Winston curled up at her feet.

The timer in the kitchen went off.

"That's the garlic bread. I'll get it." As Spencer moved past Grace, he grasped her hand for a moment.

She appreciated his attempt to reassure her.

Spencer came back with the garlic bread and sat down.

"So what's going on?" Kylie asked her dad, finally addressing the elephant in the room. "What's so big and important that we had to drive an hour for dinner on a Friday night?"

"I called you here because I wanted my family with me tonight." Spencer walked over to Grace and took her hand in his. "Grace and I wanted to share our news with all three of you as soon as possible. We've decided to get married."

There was no joy in the announcement. Only the wariness of knowing an explosion was coming.

"I knew it," Megan spat. "How could you think of replacing Mom?"

Grace couldn't believe what she was hearing. She had no intention of replacing their mother, who had passed away nearly a decade ago from cancer.

"Grace is not replacing her," Spencer insisted. "Your mother will always have a piece of my heart, but she's been gone for a long time. Grace and I love each other, and we have decided that we want to spend the rest of our lives together."

Kylie huffed and flounced back in her seat. "Well, that's ridiculous.

Did you even think of us when you made this decision? How these changes would affect your children? Or do we not matter anymore?"

Grace's jaw dropped. What in the world? She'd never seen Kylie and Megan act so childishly. She couldn't believe that they were sitting here saying that she and Spencer couldn't make decisions about their own lives without consulting their children.

"You're both adults, and you lead your own independent lives," Spencer reminded them. "Why should we have to ask your permission to get married?"

"I don't care what you say." Kylie crossed her arms. "If you guys get married, it will be one of the most selfish things you've ever done."

Spencer rested his hands on Grace's shoulders. "I don't think I've ever been ashamed of my children before. There's nothing selfish about two mature adults getting married. Grace and I have had enough grief in our lives. We've both been alone for a long time, and it's amazing that we found each other. We thought you'd be happy for us."

Grace was numb. Of all the things she'd expected to happen tonight, this was not one of them. "I will admit to being a little confused," she said to Kylie and Megan. "We've always gotten along. I don't know why you're so against this."

Megan glared at her father and Grace. "We always got along because you and Dad were friends. But this? You might not think you are, but you're trying to take our mother's place. Even when we walked in tonight, you were setting the table like you own the house. Like you already live here. You two might get married, but I'll never accept you as a stepmother. I had a mom, and no one can ever take her place."

"I'm so sorry you feel that way." Grace turned to Jake. He'd been quiet during the conversation, and she hoped it was because he didn't agree with Kylie and Megan. "You haven't said anything yet. What do you think?"

"Do you really want to get married again?" Jake asked. "Didn't you learn anything from what Dad put you through? It hasn't been that long since you found out he was alive. I have to wonder if you're on the rebound."

His words devastated her. "Yes, I do want to get married again," she said. "It's not fair to compare Spencer to your father. He would never do anything like that."

Everyone was silent as they finished their dinner. It was one of the most awkward meals Grace had ever sat through.

When it was finally over, Grace said, "I think it's time I went home."

"I'm going to walk Grace to her car," Spencer told his daughters. "I've never been so disappointed in the two of you. If I can calm down enough, we'll talk in a few minutes."

Grace couldn't even glance at Jake, Kylie, and Megan as she left the room with Spencer and Winston. She knew she wouldn't be able to hold back her tears for long. She couldn't believe how quickly the evening had deteriorated. How different she felt now than she had just a few short hours ago. Her dream of being married to Spencer lay in dust around her.

Her beautiful engagement ring was still in her pocket. She'd taken it off in expectation of putting it on again in front of the children, never dreaming of what was to happen.

Spencer ushered Grace to the car. He opened the passenger door, and Winston jumped onto the seat.

"Do you think they're right?" she asked. The tears she'd been fighting began to slide down her cheeks. "Are we being selfish?"

"We're not the selfish ones," he replied. "I can't believe my daughters would be so vicious."

Grace winced. "Jake wasn't much better. Accusing me of being on the rebound. I've been hurt before, but hearing our children tonight broke my heart."

Spencer pulled her into his arms.

As his warmth enveloped her, Grace surrendered to the anguish burning a hole in her soul. She sobbed out her grief. Not only for the pain their words had caused but also for the pain she would have to cause Spencer.

After stepping back, Grace took a tissue from her purse and wiped her eyes. Dipping her fingers into her pocket, she caught the ring and held it out to Spencer. "I can't marry you if it will cause a rift between you and your daughters. Kylie and Megan are wrong about us, but they're still your children."

"Don't be hasty," he said. "We'll work it out. Let's give them some time to get used to the idea. It'll be fine."

"Right now, I can't think beyond the agony in my heart. I love you so much. If we got married and it destroyed your relationship with your girls, it would devastate me. And it would affect us. Of course it would. How could you not resent me, knowing I caused that rift?"

"No, you didn't cause it," Spencer insisted. "Please don't do this to us. You're breaking my heart too."

When he embraced her again, Grace leaned into him, taking comfort from his strength and his love for her.

Finally, she pulled away, putting space between them. "I love you. If they ever change their minds, I'll be waiting for you. You can put the ring back on my finger then." She opened the door and slipped into the car, then drove to the inn.

When Grace walked through the front door, she hurried to her private quarters with Winston at her side. She didn't want to see anyone right now.

When Jake called her ten minutes later, she didn't answer. Instead, she switched off her phone.

Gathering Winston into her arms, she buried her face in his fur and cried for the loss of her dreams.

28

Grace

Grace woke up the next morning completely spent. She'd tossed and turned all night. It was hard to believe that she'd broken off her engagement to Spencer. But what else could she do? She wouldn't be able to live with herself if their families crumbled because of their marriage.

Grace peeked at Winston. He was curled up in his dog bed with his paw covering his eyes. She could definitely relate.

She checked her phone and found another missed call from Jake and a voice mail from Spencer. Grace sighed. She couldn't talk to either one of them right now. Her emotions were too raw.

After dragging herself out of bed, Grace showered and got dressed.

By the time she was ready, Winston was up and waiting by the door.

"Are you ready for breakfast?" she asked him.

The dog yipped.

Grace opened the door, and Winston led the way to the kitchen.

The moment she stepped into the room, Charlotte glanced up from the pot she was stirring with an expectant smile. The smile dissolved when she took in her sister's appearance. Charlotte ran over to Grace with open arms and gave her a hug.

When Charlotte pulled away, she grabbed Grace's left hand. "What happened? Where's your ring?"

Grace tried to hold back a sob, but it pushed forth as a choking sound. She hadn't thought she had any tears left.

Winnie breezed into the kitchen and stopped in her tracks when she saw her nieces. "What's the matter?"

"Grace was going to tell me what happened last night," Charlotte said.

Winston plopped down at his food bowl and whined.

"First, let me feed our little friend," Grace said. "And I could use a cup of really strong coffee. I hardly slept last night."

"Of course. Let's all have some. There's plenty." Charlotte went to the coffee maker, poured three cups, and set them on the island.

Grace filled Winston's bowl with kibble and freshened his water. After washing her hands, she collapsed onto a stool at the island.

Winnie and Charlotte sat on either side of her.

"Whatever it is, we're here for you," Winnie said, patting Grace's hand.

"Thanks. I appreciate it." Grace took a sip of coffee, then announced, "I returned the ring to Spencer." She related the disastrous evening as succinctly as possible.

"I'm so sorry." Winnie put her arm around Grace's shoulders. "I know how excited you were to share the news with the kids."

"I can't believe it," Charlotte said, sounding appalled. "I never dreamed they would react this way."

"Perhaps it was simply a shock," Winnie said. "After they have time to consider it, they'll change their minds."

"I agree," Charlotte chimed in. "Try not to worry. Things will work out for you and Spencer. You're made for each other."

Grace felt the same way. But the sinking feeling in the pit of her stomach made her wonder if it was enough.

Sam

Sam was still humming to himself as he packed again. This time it was for real. He and Alyssa had talked well into the evening. They had decided to take things slow. Now that they had confessed their feelings for each other, the tension had disappeared.

Sam was content to wait until she was ready. And on that day, he would ask her to marry him.

When he carried his suitcase to the door, he noticed a folded piece of paper on the floor. Someone had shoved it under the door. Curious, he bent down and picked it up. He opened it and read the handwritten letter.

> *Sam,*
>
> *It was good to see you this week. I realized that Wanda was right—I was being rude. I apologize.*
>
> *I noticed the way you and Alyssa were looking at each other. It's obvious I was trespassing. I hope you can forgive me.*
>
> *Congrats on winning the heart of such a great woman.*
>
> *Justin*

He folded the letter and slipped it into the side pocket of his bag. He hoped that Justin would find someone to treasure someday. It was sort of sad that he'd had to learn how his actions were affecting others the way he had, but hopefully the lesson would stick with him.

Sam left the suite with his bag and walked to the second floor. He knocked on Alyssa's door.

A few moments later, she opened the door and kissed him. Then she handed him a bag to carry out. Her eyes gleamed with laughter.

Life with her would never be dull.

Sam laughed and ushered her downstairs to the first floor.

Grace was standing behind the reception desk when they arrived. "Are you two checking out?"

"Yes, we're getting an early start," Sam replied.

Winston bounded over to them, tail wagging.

Alyssa knelt down to pet the dog. "It was a lovely time," she told Grace. "We enjoyed it."

Grace smiled. "I'm glad to hear it. We enjoyed having you. Come back anytime."

When they were checked out, they picked up the bags and walked to Sam's car.

He opened the passenger door for Alyssa.

She leaned in and kissed his cheek. "Come on. Let's go home."

Marcie

Marcie had gone to bed Friday night contemplating her career and hearing options. When she woke up Saturday morning, she realized she'd made her decisions.

Now that her mind was made up, the mental storm that had started when she lost her hearing completely had dissipated. She was at peace.

It was even more than that. She had a sense of purpose.

Excited to share her news with Charles during breakfast, Marcie took a shower and got dressed. She felt strong and bold this morning, so she picked out a cheery red lipstick to match her mood.

Pulling out her phone, she sent Allie a text letting her know she'd be home sometime in the next couple of days. Just because she was heading home didn't mean she was in a hurry. Home was still a good fifteen hours away. She wouldn't dream of making the trip in one day. Besides, she still had another week off from work.

Allie texted back almost immediately, asking if she was all right.

Marcie smiled, feeling fortunate to have such a wonderful and caring friend. *I'm getting better every day.*

What about Brian?

Over and done. No regrets.

It was true. Brian was never the man she had thought he was. She had accepted that and moved on. Even the pain he had caused her was more an embarrassing memory than an ache. Because of him, she'd almost lost the career she'd worked so hard for.

Sometimes life's lessons were difficult.

But Marcie was strong enough to handle them. She knew that now.

She promised to text Allie when she reached a stopping point on her journey so they could catch up.

When Marcie went downstairs to the dining room, excitement thrummed through her veins.

Charles and Savannah were already sitting at the table. Savannah was coloring a picture of a monkey.

Marcie ruffled Savannah's hair as she walked past her to her seat. She smiled when she noticed the cup of coffee Charles had poured for her. "You're a saint. Thank you."

"You're welcome." Charles pointed to the container of sugar on the table. "I added cream, but I decided to let you sweeten it." He smiled. "I know you like a little coffee with your sugar."

She picked up the container and poured sugar into her cup.

Charles shuddered, then took a sip of his black coffee.

Grace and Charlotte entered the room and arranged platters of eggs Benedict, sausage, bacon, and toast on the sideboard.

Marcie frowned. Grace was pale, and her eyes were puffy as if she'd been crying.

Charlotte said something to her sister, but Marcie was too far away to read her lips. Grace left the room.

"Good morning," Charlotte said as she walked over to them. "Sorry for the delay. Please help yourselves to the food."

Marcie followed Charles to the sideboard, and they filled their plates and one for Savannah.

As they ate, Marcie talked to Savannah. She was astonished to realize how many signs she knew simply by being around Savannah the past several days. They had a real conversation without Charles interpreting. That was a true improvement.

Marcie turned to Charles. "I've made some decisions."

"Really?" Charles asked. "What are they?"

"The first is that I'm going to explore the option of a cochlear implant," Marcie answered. "I grew up oral, and I think an implant would make the most sense considering my work."

She planned to contact the clinic when she got home. A cochlear implant might be an elective surgery, so she would also need to talk with the human resources department about insurance. She wasn't concerned about the financial aspect. Right now, she was merely collecting the data. When she had all the information, she'd move forward with a final decision.

"That's a good idea."

"I've also decided to stay with my law practice," Marcie said, "but it's going to change."

"How so?" he asked.

"I don't want to do corporate law anymore," Marcie replied. "I went into law school, and I loved being a lawyer at first. But I had no direction. No idea of what kind of law I wanted to practice. When Brian broke off our engagement, I got a little lost. But I've figured it out. I want to represent children and families, and I want to advocate for people who are deaf and hard of hearing."

Charles smiled. "You'll be a fantastic advocate. You're already knowledgeable about the subject matter."

"I also want to continue to learn sign language," she said. "If I'm going to represent deaf individuals, it would inspire more trust and hope if I could talk with my clients directly."

"That's definitely true," he said. "Have you thought about your next steps in learning sign language?"

"I know some people who attend events with the deaf community in my area. They've invited me to come, but I've always been too busy. Now I'm going to make time to go. I'll meet people who understand me while building my communication skills. It's a win-win situation."

"I agree," Charles said. "You've picked up a lot of signs this week. I don't think you'll have trouble learning."

"I've learned so much from talking with Savannah." Marcie got Savannah's attention and signed, "Thank you for teaching me to sign."

Savannah grinned. "I like signing with you."

Marcie curled the three middle fingers of one hand while extending the thumb and pinkie. She rocked the hand between Savannah and herself. "Me too."

Savannah made a sign that Marcie didn't recognize. Her palm faced Marcie, and the thumb, index finger, and pinkie were extended upward while the middle and ring fingers were folded down over the palm.

"I don't know that sign," Marcie admitted.

Charles cleared his throat. "That's the sign for 'I love you.'"

Marcie gasped, then gently placed her arms around Savannah and hugged her. "I love you," she signed back.

Overcome with emotion, Marcie finished her breakfast quietly.

After Charlotte cleared their empty plates, Savannah returned to her coloring, and Marcie and Charles lingered over their coffee.

"Do you have any plans this morning?" Charles asked Marcie. "I was wondering if you'd like to drive into town with us."

"Actually, I'm heading home."

"So soon?"

She nodded. "I've done what I needed to do."

Charles put his elbows on the table and folded his hands. "I hope we can see each other again. You know that there's a connection between us. I believe we're becoming good friends, and I think it may be more than that. I would like the opportunity to explore our relationship." He smiled. "And since you no longer represent me as my lawyer against my devious father-in-law, there's no more conflict of interest."

"But we live in different states," Marcie reminded him.

"Indiana and Illinois aren't that far from each other. A few hours in a car. We could easily get together on weekends. Savannah would love it too."

It sounded wonderful. "What kinds of things would we do together?"

"There are so many options," he said. "Camping, kayaking, spelunking..."

"Hang gliding," she added, just to see his reaction.

"No, I don't do heights."

She laughed. "I was only kidding."

They chatted for a little longer. Finally, Marcie couldn't put it off any longer. "I'm sorry, but I really need to go. It's time for me to head home."

"We'll see you off," Charles offered.

"I have to get my things," she said. "I'll be right back."

Marcie hurried to her room to collect her bags. It was bittersweet, but she was making the right decision. After leaving her room, she went downstairs to the reception desk.

"I hope you enjoyed your stay," Grace said as she checked her out. "Please come again."

"It was incredible. Thank you." Marcie could see that Grace wasn't herself, but she didn't pry.

Charles and Savannah were waiting on the front porch for her.

Marcie hugged Savannah goodbye. The little girl clung to her, and Marcie couldn't swallow around the lump in her throat. She was going to miss this child so much. When she finally pulled back, she brushed Savannah's tears off her cheeks.

"I love you," Marcie signed. "We'll chat on a video call. You'll see me again."

Savannah nodded. "I will miss you. I want you to come home with us."

Maybe someday, Marcie thought.

Charles knelt down in front of Savannah. "Perhaps this summer, Marcie can come out and go kayaking with us. What do you think?"

"Yay!" Savannah signed. "We can have water fights."

Marcie chuckled.

Charles stood and faced Marcie. He picked up her bag and escorted her out to her car. After stowing her bag in the trunk, he pulled her into a hug.

Marcie rested her head on his shoulder for a moment, wishing she could stay right where she was. Her heart was full.

Finally, they parted.

"I'm so happy we met," Charles said. "You've become special to both of us in such a short time."

"You and Savannah mean a lot to me as well."

"Is it okay if I text you?" he asked.

She laughed. "You have to. I just promised Savannah."

"Not Savannah. Me. I really believe our friendship could develop into more someday."

"I do too." Marcie opened her car door. "I miss you already," she blurted.

He smiled. "Me too."

He moved closer and kissed her cheek. When he backed up, their eyes met. She felt the connection in her very soul.

Marcie slid behind the wheel and reached for her seat belt. She was snapping it into place when her phone lit up with a text message.

It was from Charles, who was still standing outside her car. *I miss you. I'm not gone yet.*

Still miss you. Will you call when you get to where you're going?

She rolled down her window. "I'll text you when I reach a hotel tonight."

He nodded. "And tomorrow night."

"I will."

"And every night after that."

She smiled at the thought. Charles and Savannah wanted her in their lives. She knew that Charles would not have asked his daughter if she wanted Marcie to visit if he didn't mean it. He wouldn't want to raise her expectations.

Marcie couldn't put it off any longer. She waved and shifted her car into reverse. As she pulled out, she allowed herself one last glance at Charles and Savannah in the mirror.

While she drove away from the Magnolia Harbor Inn, Marcie dreamed of what the future might hold. She envisioned a time when she would go and visit Savannah and Charles. A time when she would be fluent in sign language and able to hold a full conversation with Savannah. There might even be a time in the not-too-distant future when she and Charles would hold hands and maybe even kiss.

Marcie felt grateful that she found out how wrong Brian was for her before she'd made a bigger mistake. A mistake that would have stopped her from meeting Charles and Savannah. A mistake that could have stopped her from discovering what she truly wanted out of life.

Unlike her drive to South Carolina, now she knew exactly where she was going and what she wanted to do when she got there.

Marcie hadn't kept up with her journal in weeks. Now she couldn't wait to write down her new plan in it. She had finally learned what really mattered in her life.

Charles and Savannah would be at the top of her daily lists.

31

Grace

Grace couldn't focus. She was exhausted from her lack of sleep last night, and she hadn't been able to finish her breakfast.

Winston sensed her distress and remained at her side. The dog occasionally leaned against her legs, offering his silent support.

Every time she thought of Spencer, it felt like her heart was breaking all over again. She felt guilty because she hadn't responded to his message yet. But what could she possibly say? She couldn't be the wedge that came between him and his daughters. He might deny it, but she knew it would destroy him. If his family were broken, someday he would grow to resent Grace, and that would devastate her.

Jake had called her again too, but she'd let it go to voice mail. She couldn't talk to him right now either. She couldn't talk to anyone.

Grace held out hope that someday their children would accept them as a couple, but right now it was very difficult not to feel bitter or betrayed. Even toward her own son.

Her only solace was in keeping busy. After freshening the guest rooms, she went to the barn to clean up after the conference. She scrubbed tables, took down banners and streamers, and picked up trash while Winston supervised.

The Christmas tree twinkling in the corner of the barn seemed to mock her bleak mood. She had been so excited about gathering with her loved ones during the holidays. Christmas was supposed to be a time of joy. A time of hope.

Grace had neither.

Winston put his front paws on her knees as if begging her to be happy.

Grateful for the sweet dog, she reached down and petted him.

When Grace finished putting the barn back to rights, she switched off the lights and closed the door.

As she and Winston headed to the inn, she spotted Spencer striding toward them. She blinked to make sure she wasn't dreaming. For a moment, hope beat wildly against her rib cage, but it died when he got closer and she saw his expression. He wasn't coming to tell her that his daughters had changed their minds.

"I've come to ask you to reconsider," Spencer said.

She could hardly bear to look at him, understanding his pain as she did. "I want to run off and get married right now. But I can't be the person who destroys your family. That would hurt you too much."

"This is hurting me too. I love you. There is nothing I want more than to spend my life with you."

Tears clouded her eyes. "I love you too. I keep hoping that maybe those stubborn children of ours will come around and realize what they've done."

He winced.

"Have you talked to them yet?" Grace asked, wringing her hands.

"Not since they left last night," Spencer replied. "I told them not to call me for a few days. I'm too hurt and angry to talk to them rationally. I know they don't see it this way, but I feel as though they've betrayed me."

"And that's why we have to wait." She gazed into the distance. "Once these bad feelings die down, hopefully they'll see our point of view."

"Have you spoken to Jake?"

"He called a few times, but I haven't responded. I can't deal with him right now." Grace sighed. "I should get back to the inn."

"I'll walk with you," he offered.

They ambled to the inn with Winston leading the way.

When they reached the back door, Spencer said, "I love you. I won't return the ring to the jewelry store because I plan to put it back on your finger, where it belongs."

Grace desperately wanted to believe his words. "I love you too."

She watched his shoulders slump as he walked away. He appeared to be weighed down by a heavy burden. It was a burden that had been placed upon them both by their children.

Grace and Winston entered the mansion and made a detour to the kitchen.

Charlotte hurried over to Grace and embraced her. "How are you doing?"

"Spencer stopped by," Grace said. "He asked me to reconsider."

"What did you tell him?" Charlotte asked.

She sank onto a stool at the island and related their conversation. "I can't be responsible for conflict between him and his daughters."

"I can't imagine how difficult this is," Charlotte said, sounding concerned. "Can I get you something to eat? You hardly touched your breakfast."

"No thanks. I'm not hungry."

"I'm not taking no for an answer. You need to keep your strength up." Charlotte marched to the fridge and removed a few items. "A nice salad is just what the chef ordered."

Winston yipped in agreement.

"See? You're outnumbered." Charlotte quickly assembled the salad and topped it with her homemade vinaigrette. She poured a glass of lemonade, retrieved a fork and a napkin, and set everything in front of her sister.

"Thanks," Grace said. She took a bite. "It's delicious."

"Of course it is," Charlotte said with a grin. She glanced down at Winston. "Don't worry. I haven't forgotten about you." She grabbed a doggie biscuit from the cabinet and gave it to him.

Winston plopped down on the floor and began crunching on it.

Although Grace didn't have much of an appetite, she managed to finish her lunch. "Thanks again."

"Anytime." Charlotte cleared Grace's dishes, then wrapped her in a hug. "Why don't you go to your quarters and rest? I have everything under control. Besides, the new guests aren't arriving until tomorrow."

"That sounds wonderful," Grace said. "I feel a headache coming on."

Charlotte handed her sister a bottle of ibuprofen and a glass of water. "If you need anything else, let me know."

"Thanks." Grace swallowed the pills, then drank the water. She hoped it would dull the pain throbbing behind her eyes.

Grace walked to her quarters, Winston jogging faithfully at her side. She immediately climbed into bed.

Winston curled up in his bed.

When she woke up an hour later, she felt lethargic, but her headache was gone.

Her phone buzzed, and she grabbed it off the nightstand. It was an e-mail letting her know that the Christmas gift she'd ordered for Spencer had been shipped.

Fresh tears sprang to her eyes, and she set the phone down.

Winston jumped into bed beside her, and she snuggled him close.

There was a light knock on her door.

Assuming it was her sister, Grace called, "Come in."

But it was Jake who entered the room. "I was worried when you didn't answer my calls. Are you all right?"

Sudden anger rose inside her. How dare he ask her that? She raised her hands and brushed away the tears. As she dropped her hands to her lap, she noticed Jake staring at her.

"Didn't Spencer give you an engagement ring?" he asked, sounding anxious.

"Yes, but I gave it back," Grace answered.

Jake's face paled. "You broke off your engagement because of what we said?"

"What did you think I was going to do? You know me. How was I supposed to marry Spencer knowing it was going to damage his relationship with his daughters? I couldn't do that to him."

"What about what Dad put you through?" he asked. "Do you really want to get married again?"

"Yes, I do. Your father was gone for a long time, and I finally found someone I deeply love. Spencer and I want to spend our lives together. We were excited to share the news with our children, and we thought you'd be happy for us. Instead, you tell me that I'm on the rebound, and Spencer's daughters claim that we're selfish for not wanting to be alone. Selfish because we didn't ask our children's opinion about how we should spend the last years of our lives."

"I was worried that you were jumping into another marriage after what happened with Dad," Jake admitted. "And I guess I never thought how you must've felt all those years after he was gone."

"You're my son, and I love you very much," Grace said. "But there's room in my life for more than you. I don't want to be alone now that Spencer and I have found each other. I'm sorry if you and Kylie and Megan find this hard to understand. But what you did was wrong."

She gently set Winston aside, got out of bed, and paced the room. "You three decided that your opinions about our relationship are more important than our happiness."

Jake walked over to her and hugged her close. "I'm sorry. I didn't mean for this to happen. You're the last person I would ever want to see unhappy. Please forgive me."

They stood, wrapped in each other's arms, for several long minutes. Grace could feel the strength of his regret and sorrow through their embrace. She knew that her son was speaking the truth. Just as she knew that if he could undo the harm he caused, he would.

Unfortunately, it was impossible to take back the words now that they'd been spoken. There was no way to fix what they had done until they accepted Spencer and Grace as a couple. Until that happened, Grace couldn't marry Spencer.

"I want to apologize to Spencer too," Jake said as he stepped back.

"I'm sure he'll appreciate it," she said.

He sat down on the bed and scratched behind Winston's ears. "Can I still stay here until after Christmas?"

"Of course you can," Grace replied. "The Wisteria Loft Suite is yours."

"I'm going to call Spencer," Jake said. He gave Grace another hug before he left the room.

She was glad that Jake apologized, but apparently he hadn't changed his mind about their marriage. She feared that their children would never accept their relationship.

Maybe Grace and Spencer weren't meant for each other after all.

Grace went through the next few days in a fog. She struggled to smile for Charlotte and Winnie and their new guests, but she knew she didn't fool them.

Jake spent most of the time with his old friends. Grace mainly saw him during breakfast. He didn't talk about what she had said to him. It was as if the whole conversation had never happened.

She heard nothing from Spencer, and she couldn't blame him. Grace had turned him down when he'd asked her to reconsider. She had no idea if his daughters had talked to him about what had happened or not. If Spencer contacted Grace, she knew it would only open the wound more.

She was certain that he would keep his promise to her and hold on to her ring until things changed.

If they changed.

On Tuesday, three days before Christmas, the gift Grace had so eagerly ordered for Spencer arrived. As she opened the package, a few more tears fell, but mostly she felt numb. With gentle fingers, she assembled the gift. Lovingly she wrapped it up for Spencer, as if she would be able to give it to him on Christmas Day.

When it was wrapped, she placed it under the little Christmas tree in her private quarters. It sat there alone.

Just as she was.

32

Grace

Grace normally reveled in the holidays. She enjoyed the decorations, the lavish feasts, and the joy she felt from spending time with her friends and family.

But this Christmas Eve, she was overcome by sadness. A few short days ago, she'd had such high expectations. Grace and Spencer should have been planning their wedding. She had envisioned them celebrating their upcoming nuptials and the holidays, surrounded by their joyful, supportive families. Instead, she was sitting in her private quarters with Winston, feeling sorry for herself.

Winston didn't fuss when she held him tighter. Her dog seemed to sense that she needed the comfort.

She hadn't seen Jake since yesterday morning. She knew he felt terrible about his part in breaking up her engagement. She forgave him, but that awful dinner with Spencer's daughters and Jake still bothered her.

Instinctively, she glanced at her finger. It was amazing how much she missed her engagement ring. It had been on her hand for only two days.

Grace knew it wasn't the ring she missed. It was Spencer. She missed his laugh. She missed his sense of humor and his kindness. She missed his strong arms wrapped around her shoulders. Come to think of it, there wasn't anything about him that she didn't miss.

Someone knocked on the door, interrupting her reverie.

"Come in," Grace said, even though she wasn't feeling up to company.

Charlotte poked her head into the room. "Winnie and I made lunch, and I baked a cake. I went a little overboard, and there's far too much food here for the two of us. You should join us in the dining room."

Lunch sounded good, but Grace hesitated. "I thought you had a date with Dean."

She would hate it if Charlotte had canceled her date to stay home and keep her company. She was the older sister. She was the one who was supposed to take care of Charlotte, not the other way around.

"I do, but it's not until tonight. We have plenty of time." Charlotte raised her eyebrows. "Are you coming?"

"You've convinced me," Grace said. "Can you give me twenty minutes?"

"See you then." Charlotte closed the door and left.

Grace sighed. Now she had to get dressed and sit and laugh with her sister and her aunt. But they would understand that she was feeling low. They always understood. She didn't know how she'd make it through this current crisis without them.

She chided herself. This wasn't like her. She was tired of holding her own pity party.

After taking a shower, she went to her closet and searched for a festive outfit to wear. After all, it was Christmas Eve. Grace blinked back tears. She refused to cry anymore.

Grace picked out a silky green dress that shimmered and paired it with sparkly silver heels.

Checking the mirror, she frowned at her reflection. She was a mess. Her cheeks were pale, and she had dark circles under her eyes. She'd lost five pounds in the past few days, making the dress too loose and deepening the hollows below her cheekbones.

Grace definitely needed makeup today. She tried to hide her paleness with foundation, then applied a coat of mascara, some blush, and a neutral shade of lipstick.

Standing back, she examined the results. The concealer masked some of the dark circles, but it didn't completely obliterate them. She still wasn't at her best, but at least it was an improvement.

"Come on, Winston. Charlotte and Winnie have requested our presence."

Winston seemed to sense her mood. He came and leaned against her leg, as if holding her up with his small body.

"Thanks for the support, buddy. I need all I can get."

Grace opened the door, and they strode toward the dining room. She could hear Charlotte and Winnie. Their voices sounded cheerful, but they were slightly subdued. Guilt nagged at her. They were subdued because of her. Her compassionate sister and aunt hurt when she did.

As Grace and Winston walked into the room, Winnie stood and met her with open arms.

As Winnie's warmth and love enveloped her, she bit her lip. She wouldn't cry. Not today. If she did, they'd feel even worse for her. She hugged Winnie back, then eased out of the embrace.

Charlotte swooped in and gave Grace a hug.

"If you two make me cry, my mascara will run," Grace warned. "Then bad things will happen."

The women laughed.

"Sit down," Winnie said, gesturing to the table laden with food. "We made a feast."

"Charlotte always makes a feast," Grace reminded her.

"It's better to be prepared," Charlotte said. She gently ushered her sister to one of the chairs.

Grace sat down and regarded the offerings. There were platters of turkey and stuffing, mashed potatoes and gravy, green bean casserole, and other traditional holiday dishes. She didn't know how much she'd be able to eat, but she'd try. Her sister had truly gone above and beyond with this meal.

Charlotte, however, wasn't done. She brought out several more dishes and arranged them on the table.

"Everything looks wonderful as always," Grace remarked. "But that's an awful lot of food for only the three of us."

Winnie's expression was suspiciously innocent. She knew something. What had the two of them planned to cheer her up?

Jake popped into the room. "Is it all right that I invited some friends over?"

"Of course," Charlotte said as she scanned the array of food. "We have plenty."

Grace narrowed her eyes and wondered what was going on.

"Good," Jake said. "Because we're starving."

Grace spun around and saw Spencer, Kylie, Megan, Gus, and Dean standing in the doorway. She dropped her napkin, jumped to her feet, and raced across the room. Without thinking about it, she hurled herself into Spencer's arms.

Spencer held her close, and she could feel him trembling against her.

When he leaned away from her, he traced her cheekbones. "You're not eating or sleeping, are you?"

Grace stifled a sigh. Her efforts to hide behind makeup hadn't worked. She peered at him. "You haven't had an easy week either."

"It's been rough," Spencer admitted. "But it's about to get better." He glanced at his daughters.

"We want to apologize," Kylie said to Grace. "When Dad announced your engagement, Megan and I were angry."

"But after you left, Jake said he'd never seen you so devastated," Megan added. "We felt bad about that."

"You didn't sound like you felt bad," Spencer commented.

"We were being stubborn," Kylie admitted. "We were the selfish ones, not the two of you. We'd gotten used to Dad being able to drop everything when we needed him. And sometimes when we didn't."

"Jake told us off," Megan said, "and he was totally right."

Surprised, Grace turned to her son. "You did?"

Jake shrugged. "I thought it was telling that they said it was selfish that you hadn't consulted them because it would change their lives. None of us really paid attention when Spencer said that you two had both suffered and been alone long enough."

Megan walked over to Grace. "I had an amazing mother, but now I'm an adult. I don't need someone to raise me anymore. But I sincerely like you, and I can see how important you are to Dad. I think it would be wonderful if you married Dad and we were friends."

Kylie joined her sister. "Jake told us that you'd broken your engagement with Dad because you didn't want to come between us. That made me realize just how small-minded I'd been. I'll regret hurting you and Dad for the rest of my life. Please, Grace, can you forgive us?"

Grace stepped away from Spencer to hug Kylie and Megan. All three of them were crying when she released them. After regaining her composure, Grace managed to choke out, "I forgive you both."

"Do you still love me enough to take my ring back?" Spencer knelt down on one knee in front of her. "Grace, will you marry me?"

"Yes." Grace dropped to her knees in front of Spencer and kissed him, letting him know how much she loved him. She poured her heart and soul into the kiss.

The others cheered and applauded. Winston raced in circles, yipping. Everyone laughed at the dog's antics.

"Okay, let's eat before the food gets cold," Charlotte ordered.

Spencer slipped the ring on Grace's finger where it belonged, then helped her to her feet. She leaned against his arm, dizzy with joy. Side by side, they moved to the table. Spencer pulled out her chair.

Everyone took their seats and passed around the food. Grace's appetite returned with a vengeance. She savored the tasty dishes as they all talked and laughed together. It felt so good to laugh again.

As lunch was wrapping up, Grace remembered something. She jumped to her feet and hurried to the door. "I'll be right back."

Grace rushed to her quarters and snatched the package under the Christmas tree. Hugging it to her chest, she returned to the others.

Spencer left the table and came to her. "Is everything all right?"

"Yes, everything is fine." She smiled. "I know that tomorrow is Christmas, but this seems like an appropriate time to give you a present. I thought I'd never be able to give it to you. I don't know why I wrapped it." She handed the present to her fiancé.

Spencer carefully unwrapped the gift. When he saw what it was, he hugged her.

"What is it?" Megan called.

Silently, he rotated the frame in his hands so that everyone could see the picture inside it.

It was the picture Charlotte had taken of Spencer and Grace the day after he asked her to marry him. Spencer had his arm around her shoulders. Grace held the beautiful bouquet of roses, and the light caught the engagement ring, making it sparkle.

There was no way anyone looking at the picture would doubt that they were two people deeply in love. It was a perfect moment.

"What a great photo," Kylie remarked.

Everyone agreed.

"Is anyone ready for dessert?" Charlotte asked as she cleared the table.

The others groaned.

"I'm ready," Gus said.

"Maybe we should wait a little while before we indulge," Winnie suggested, then playfully nudged her husband.

"Good idea," Spencer said. He stood and held out his arm to Grace. "Would you care to accompany me on a walk?"

"I'd be delighted." She rose and took his arm.

"We'll be back in time for dessert," Spencer told the others before they left the room.

Grace laughed. "You and your sweet tooth."

As they walked out the front door and headed toward the lake, they talked about the events of the day.

"Are Kylie and Megan really okay with our marriage?" Grace asked.

"They are. And even more, I think they're sincerely ashamed of their behavior. Trust me, that issue has been put to rest." He paused. "You impressed them."

"Me?" she asked, startled. She'd done nothing but go home and cry.

Spencer nodded. "When they realized what they'd done, they also understood that you had put their needs ahead of your own desires even after they had treated you so horribly. That made them feel the weight of how badly they had misjudged you."

"You told them why I returned the ring?"

"No, that was Jake. He contacted them after he talked to you. He told me it wouldn't do any good for us to get engaged if my girls were going to continue to fuss about it."

Grace rested her head against his arm. "Giving your ring back was the hardest thing I've ever done. I honestly thought I could feel my heart shattering inside my chest."

"Well, mine got bruised that night too." He kissed the top of her head. "I kept the ring on me at all times. I knew I would do whatever I had to in order to get it back on your finger."

She drew in a deep breath. "It's over now. This ring is mine, and I'm never giving it back to you."

"I wouldn't accept it." Spencer grinned. "You're stuck with me."

"And I couldn't be happier," Grace said. "Now we can start planning our wedding."

"And tomorrow, we can spend our first Christmas together as a couple."

"I love the sound of that."

When it started getting chilly, Spencer and Grace returned to the inn and entered the dining room.

Charlotte was in the midst of slicing a rich chocolate cake. She grinned at them. "You're just in time for dessert."

Winnie arranged Christmas cookies on a platter, and Jake refilled the glasses.

Grace and Spencer joined the others at the table.

Grace had thought she was too full to eat anything else, but when the desserts were passed around, she took a small piece of cake and a cookie.

Winston whined.

"I made special cookies for you," Charlotte told the dog as she gave him one.

Winston wagged his tail as he crunched on the treat.

As Grace enjoyed the desserts and the lively conversation around her, she glanced around the table and smiled at her family. What a blessing to gather with the people she held dear to celebrate the holiday and their engagement.

Their loved ones had been reunited, and Grace and Spencer were getting married. She had so much to be thankful for on this special Christmas Eve.

Up to this point, we've been doing all the writing. Now it's *your* turn!

Tell us what you think about this book, the characters, the plot, or anything else you'd like to share with us about this series. We can't wait to hear from *you*!

Log on to give us your feedback at:
https://www.surveymonkey.com/r/MagnoliaHarbor

Annie's FICTION